# The Travels and Travails of Stella Bellamy

Barbara Schreiner

Ralph Iron Publishers, Pretoria, South Africa 2018



The Travels and Travails of Stella Bellamy
© 2018 by Barbara Schreiner



For information regarding permission, email the publisher at barbaraschreinerz@gmail.com, subject line: Permission.

ISBN- print: 978-0-6399835-0-9
ISBN- electronic: 978-0-6399835-1-6

Book and cover design by Caryatid Design

# Beating the Cow

Who sees the pics of her rumpled, post-flight face through the windscreen of a somewhat battered Toyota, as the cameras above the A104 into Nairobi flash and flash? Is some tired and paranoid Kenyan official poring over instantaneous, if grainy, versions of her face? Do the digital images stop in Kenya, or is some CIA face-recognition software at this very moment analysing them, tagging her as a regular, if not very attractive, visitor? Does the software link to her Facebook, LinkedIn, Twitter accounts? Trigger a search through her endless emails, even the spam? Or has the bored Kenyan securocrat already dismissed her as largely irrelevant to Kenyan or global security?

Probably the latter, Stella thinks. It's the mantra of my life. Largely irrelevant.

She sighs. It's something she does often these days. How long had it been since she gave up her dance with life and started to plod, looking out on the world with sad eyes behind trying-to-be-modern glasses?

The driver's eyes flick left and right in silence, watching the traffic. And, absurdly, her mood lightens. What the hell, she's alive, in a foreign country. Who knows what adventures might await …

This is not the kind of adventure she had in mind.

She feels like an actress in a 1970s film noir. The scene, black and white, grainy, is set upstairs, where, in a double bed draped in shabby mosquito netting, a pudgy, middle-aged woman lies spread-eagled against the heat, cellulite glistening with a faint sheen of perspiration. Her grey and low-lighted hair in disarray, her eyes are fixed on the curtains as if staring might bleach their smog-yellow glow to something less insalubrious.

In the kitchen below a bald and very dark-skinned chef, pounds a chunk of Kenya's not-quite-best beef into submission – *boemf, boemf, boemf* – each sweaty thump reverberates through the cement-block walls and into the woman's tired-and-wired brain.

Outside, vast flocks of grimy black and white marabou storks, figments of Daphne du Maurier's worst nightmare, have surrendered their ghastly sentinel watch on Nairobi's buildings and settled into their shit-encrusted tumbles of sticks, their gizzards rotten with municipal dump delicacies.

Night-time in Nairobbery, thinks Stella. What a movie. My head is throbbing to the sound of a chef pulverising steak. It's hot as hell. There are holes in the mosquito netting big enough for bats to fly through.

What a day. Thirty minor government officials sweated through the challenges of climate change for decision-making while the groaning air-conditioner failed to address the present climate, let alone any future, warmer option. Hot flushes had turned to trickles of perspiration down the back of her neck.

Civil servants are risk-averse. They like plans, budgets, outcomes, key performance indicators and clear objectives. They like certainty. Which climate change has swept away.

The best they can hope for is to make a plan when massive droughts or floods hit – the impacts of climate change caused by the materialistic over-consumption of people half a world away.

The worry was evident on thirty faces – well twenty-eight, one was on his cell phone most of the day and one seemed to be watching a movie on his tablet – when she explained that models can't predict exactly *how* rainfall will change, only that it *will* change. And that it *will* get hotter. And that poor, afflicted Africa, despite having done little or nothing to cause climate change, will get hotter than anywhere else. A hotter climate means more extreme events. More intense floods. More intense droughts. And more bloody hot flushes. Changes in rainfall patterns and timing. But how much, and where?

Only the goddesses, made angry by the demands of humans, know that.

Not that she said that to her eager students, just that nothing can predict accurately how rainfall will change. The practical response is to accept the uncertainty. Nothing new in that. Life has always been unpredictable, called to order by our desperate need to plan. It was tiring, taking them through a new way of thinking about the future. Perhaps some of them got it. But she doubts whether she conveyed her message well, whether her case studies were sufficiently relevant. Doubts, as usual, her effectiveness.

Stella reaches for her glass of gin, but it is empty and the ice has melted. Even the glass is warm.

At least the cocktail party was fun, she thinks, remembering Meshack describe his attempts to stop a truckload of illegal charcoal heading from Nyakweri forest to South Sudan.

'I'm standing next to the truck, and I ask these men where do they think they are going and where did they get this charcoal? It's just me. And three men in the truck. They look at me, very cross. I'm hoping they don't have guns. I tell them to get out of the car and show me their identity documents. Just when they get out of the car, five lions come round the corner, down the road towards us. These city boys, they jump on top of the charcoal on their truck. Don't they know how lions can jump? Me? I see the keys are still in the ignition so I get into the truck and I drive them, on top of the charcoal, to the police station and I charge them with illegal charcoal selling. I tell them, those lions, they're on my side, tell your friends not to come to steal wood here. Me and my lions, we'll catch them every time!'

She drifts off to the remembered sound of raucous laughter when another steak is ordered. *Boemf, boemf, boemf.*

Fuck! She feels the prickles start under her skin, the signal of an impending hot flush. Double fuck.

At 3:30 the next afternoon, Stella drags herself away from her workshop report and into the shower. Tepid water trickles from the ancient showerhead and then, as if a switch has flipped, bursts through in a scalding cascade. The Nairobi traffic is legendary, so she's given herself four hours to get to the airport before her flight departs, has checked in online, and only has a cabin bag to take with her. It's all in hand. Except that this is Nairobi, and Njiraini, the highly recommended taxi driver, is 'just ten minutes away' for the next two hours, arriving at 5:30 in a veteran Toyota Corolla held together by rust and hope.

Njiraini thumps the boot open with his fist and tosses her bag in amongst a turmoil of old newspapers, plastic packets and a t-shirt that once celebrated *uhuru* but now wipes grease from his hands after the many, many times he fiddles under the hood to keep his *skorokoro* on the road.

Stella leaps in, as much as her flabby ageing body will allow her to, sinks into the sagging embrace of broken springs and motions impatiently to Njiraini to hurry. He leans in to open his door from the inside, the outside handle having departed for somewhere better, and eases himself onto the cracked plastic of the seat as if scared that too much enthusiasm might plunge both the seat and his lanky frame through the floor and onto the baking tarmac.

The car starts on the third try, while Stella takes deep yoga breaths to control her irritation. They putter towards the elaborate gate that guards the conference centre, where she hands over a stamped, certified copy of her laptop's make and serial number. The security officer, in crisp black uniform and white gloves, despite the heat, takes the paper with superb indifference. His animated conversation with a large woman who sells sweets from a blue plastic basin doesn't break a beat as he waves them through into the mêlée of rush-hour pedestrians, cars and hooting *matatus*.

Njiraini negotiates past potholes that could hide a hippopotamus and into the stream of traffic on Tika road. The four hours has shrunk to less than two. Stella wills herself to relax, until, without warning, Njiraini hits a hard left onto a road, so extraneous to the flow of the city, that the tar is scattered like freckles amidst mud and large puddles of water, in the middle of which, a mange-ridden mongrel scratches for fleas.

'What now?'

'Better car,' mutters Njiraini as he pulls up alongside a marginally newer white Toyota. Like something in the getaway scene of a *skop, skiet en donner* movie, he tosses her suitcase into the boot of the other car and bundles her, without a word, into the passenger seat. The new driver, who introduces himself with a broad smile as Jomo, launches them back onto Tika road.

And a war of attrition begins: can he squeeze the car into a non-existent gap between trucks, buses, cars – a gap created by sheer willpower. He is relentless. Even matatu drivers give way in the face of his determination.

Stella drops her head back against the headrest and closes her eyes, the push, shove and weave beyond stressful. A bump rips open her eyes. She clutches at her seat belt. They're on the shoulder as Jomo overtakes, (or is it undertakes) a long line of trucks on the left, over the rumble strips designed to stop people doing this. They squeeze between the massive wheels of a cattle truck and the edge of the road where the tar breaks away to mud and a steep drop down to a row of shacks. She closes her eyes and breathes into the pit of her stomach, searching for calm.

Breathe, Stella, breathe. To her relief, the bumps stop. The ride is smooth again.

She risks opening her eyes and they freeze open in dismay. Jomo is overtaking a solid line of traffic, as a monstrous truck bears down on them. Just as she is about to scream, and her right foot hits an imaginary brake, Jomo conjures up a gap between a construction truck and a brightly painted bus and they slip out of the line of death. Stella draws a deep, ragged breath and shuts her eyes again.

She staggers into the airport an hour later; her hands shake and she wants a gin and tonic with a passion, but there is no time. She runs to the Ethiopian Airways counter, dragging her battered suitcase behind her. She is convinced that she has missed the plane but determined to get on it. She cannot face the trip back into town to find a hotel for the night. Sweat runs down her neck and between her breasts from a combination of heat, hurry and hot flushes.

A composed young woman behind the counter smiles at her with a tinge of sadness. 'The flight is closed, ma'am.'

'I'm already checked in.'

The smile brightens. 'Only cabin bag?'

'Only cabin bag.'

'Quickly to the gate. Run. They let you on.'

Bugger it, Stella thinks as she hurries down the dim passageway with its peeling, once yellow paint. I'm too old to be running through airports. Too old, and too fat. And these shoes are blistering my toes.

She squeezes her computer bag into a packed overhead locker and scrambles into the window seat over a stout woman in a shiny floral dress. The woman clutches a bulky, *faux* ostrich skin handbag on her lap.

Wonderful, thinks Stella, feeling the fleshy pressure of the woman's arms oozing over the armrest, the glamour of international travel. Her seatbelt clipped into place, she squeezes up against the window and begins to relax, the thought of the drinks trolley starting a small smile at the corners of her mouth.

The floral extravaganza next to her sends texts to Rev Jerry as if Doomsday were approaching. Her thumbs move with the dexterity of a Russian concert pianist playing Chopin in the Royal Albert Hall.

No, thinks Stella, not Chopin. Too subtle. Beethoven. Or Wagner.

Despite the 'Please turn off all electronic equipment' barked from the speakers above them, the texting continues. Clearly, Mama Concert Pianist's messages are more important than passenger safety. Maybe she knows she has a personal saviour looking after her.

*Amen, Rev Jerry, and thanks for making me feel so welcome.* Stella reads over the rotund shoulder, reckoning that if Mama Concert Pianist can ignore safety instructions, she, Stella, can ignore common politeness. *I am blessed to know you. There is no answer from Rev Jerry — it is all one-way traffic. I will be back soon. May the Lord bless you, Rev.*

'Please turn off your phone, ma'am.' The air hostess is young and elegant in a traditional white Ethiopian dress, trimmed with green and gold. But she is no match for Mama CP, who holds her phone face down on her knee until the threat has moved away and starts again. *Rev Peter, thanks so much for the wisdom and prayer.*

How many Reverends does this woman know? By now both Stella and the man in 7C are glaring at her and her phone, but she is wrapped in a cocoon of righteousness. It is only when they taxi down the runway that she turns off the phone with obvious reluctance, reaches into her voluminous handbag, pulls out a second phone and turns it off, reaches back into her bag, pulls out a tablet and turns that off.

Either Mama CP's imaginary friend is working overtime, or the pilot is good at his job because they lift off into the air without mishap and rise high above Nairobi, the patchwork of houses, traffic, and green and brown fields way below them.

Within minutes, Mama CP is asleep. Her slack mouth emits intermittent grunts and snores. Stella blocks out the noise with headphones and classical music, but they don't help with the elbow war. As she slips deeper into sleep, Mama CP settles like a jelly on a warm day. Her arm swells towards Stella, who retracts like a snail's horn until she can retract no further. Then she retaliates – a quick jab of her elbow into the soft flesh. For a minute, the arm retracts and then begins its slow slide back. Jab. Pause. Slide. Jab. And so it goes.

Until Mama CP speaks. 'Madam, you are jerking me awake.'

'You're in my space,' mumbles Stella, embarrassed to have the elbow war manifested in speech. Some things are best not spoken of.

'No, madam, I am not in your space. You are poking me.'

Stella pushes the earphones deeper into her ears and retreats into pretend sleep, huddled against the window.

Another few hours, she thinks, plus the stop in Addis, that's all. Hours of hell. Hell is being trapped on a plane with no place to go. The arm next to her swells and swells.

Over a pre-dawn breakfast, Stella thaws. Her curiosity overrides the arm wrestling of the previous night.

'Did you get some sleep?' she smiles at Mama CP, who is gracious, Christian even, in her response.

'Yes, thank you. I slept fine.' Stella pauses while Mama CP bows her head over nauseating yellow eggs and luminous pink yoghurt.

'Where are you going?'

A slightly unstable yellow forkful pauses midway to her mouth.

'To Mumbai,' smiles Mama CP with joy in her voice. 'I have been studying the Bible with Reverend Jerry, and now I am taking everything I learned back to our mission there.'

Africans taking Christianity to India? muses Stella, How the world has changed.

'I have been so blessed,' continues Mama CP, now on a roll. 'What church do you attend?'

Stella fills her mouth with pink yoghurt but Mama CP waits, beaming.

'I don't,' mutters Stella, and waits for the wrath of god to strike her dead.

The fork quivers. 'Now you are giving me a complicated answer,' says Mama CP. 'What do you mean?'

'I don't go to church.'

The fork shakes. 'Why not?'

'Because I am not religious.'

'This is getting even more complicated.'

'Actually,' ventures Stella, 'it's quite simple. I don't go to church because I don't believe in god.'

Silence ices through the plane. Voices fall silent, and frozen seconds stretch into a tundra of minutes. Stella scrapes out the last of the now nearly frozen yoghurt, chastised.

At length, Mama CP speaks again. 'Then what do you do for spirituality?'

Stella is stumped.

'What happens to your spirit when you die? Your holy soul?' Mama CP persists.

Oh. That spirituality? 'I don't think I have a soul. When I die, that's it. It's over.'

Mama CP tut-tuts in distress. Stella muses that her only hope for life after death will be when her atoms enter the food chain through the mouths of maggots and bacteria (not that bacteria have mouths) to drift up and down through one life form or another.

'But when you die the priest will be there?'

'Nope.'

'But when you got married, the priest was there?'

Oh dear, thinks Stella, deeper into the bog with every step. 'I'm not married.'

'Not married?' Mama CP's voice has gone up half an octave and could reach to the back of a very large evangelical church. 'No husband? No children?' Her hands fiddle with the detritus of breakfast. 'What do you do without the ten commandments?

How do you know what is right without the word of God?'

Stella sighs. Here we go again. 'You don't have to be religious to have a moral code. I know what's right and wrong. It's quite simple – do as you would be done by. As simple as that.'

'Hm,' says Mama CP, evidently deeply suspicious. 'I'll pray for you.' And she closes her eyes in defence against the proximity of a heretic.

Stella waves to the air hostess. 'Coffee, please. Strong. One sugar.' She stretches her legs and gazes at her ankles in dismay. She's lost them again. They've vanished into plump blobs of aeroplane-induced oedema. Awesome, she thinks, my belly fat just shared itself with my ankles. How sexy!

# The Old Man at the Gate

It's good to be home. Even the sound of a voice from the gate, which interrupts her cooking, feels good. Another beggar, Stella thinks, too happy to be back in her own space to feel pissed off. It's a steady stream of people asking for handouts. But this one is different. It's the old man. She knows him well.

She's used to his cheerful wave when she drives past where he sits on the pavement, hoping for a piece-job, his small packet of possessions at his feet. It lifts her mood as if she has a friend in the neighbourhood.

She hands over a packet of bananas, apples, a tin of beans *chakalaka* and an old Fanta bottle filled with tap water. She smiles. He smiles back, warm eyes in a dark face.

'I'm getting my pension next month, Mama. Next month it is coming for sure.' She is grateful that he calls her mama, not madam. It reduces the distance between them. She likes him for that. And for his grace in growing old, despite his poverty. She wishes she had as much grace, as much warmth in her smile. It's true, she thinks, money can't buy you happiness. It makes living more comfortable, but happiness is something else.

Something he has. Something she has lost.

'Excellent, that's very good.'

'Two hundred thousand Rand I must put it in the bank so I can get the interest.'

Stella launches into an explanation of interest rates and investment opportunities, how he must ask the bank for the best investment, concerned that he will put it in a savings account where interest is lower than inflation. He smiles and nods. She tells him again to take the money straight to the bank and to ask them to advise him on how to invest it. He wants to know how much interest they will pay him each month. 'They don't pay it monthly,' she answers, 'only once a year. You'll get about ten thousand Rand a year. Maybe a bit more.'

And she smiles, and he smiles, and they part, each pretending that there really is a pension, that his life will change for the better; that this isn't just a story that keeps him hopeful and her talking; that appeases his hunger with hope.

She wonders about his history. He's never drunk, always neat, in the same brown trousers and worn corduroy jacket. She wonders if he has a room somewhere that shields him at night, or a piece of pavement and a sheet of cardboard. Wonders where he comes from, where his family is, what brought him to her gate all those months ago, asking for food and water.

One day perhaps she'll ask him. She might even ask his name.

# Stirrings of Desire

It's lunchtime at the provincial workshop on water pricing when Stella is caught unawares by a sudden upsurge of desire. Haroon gestures for her to step in front of him in the queue. The long brown fingers and taut muscle stretching back from his wrist make her skin prickle. She realises how long it's been since she was touched with tenderness. She's excited by his intellect, energised by how he synthesizes disparate ideas into something new, something she would not have thought of. She didn't expect her response to be so visceral.

She glances surreptitiously at his hand, hoping to see whether he wears a wedding ring, knowing that any absence might mean only that he doesn't wear one, not that he is single. She snorts mockingly at herself. He's sure to be married, she thinks. Most of the good ones are. Or gay. These days they're gay and married.

She loads olives and feta cheese onto her plate. She wonders what his beard would feel like against her cheek. Sexy, or just scratchy? It's been so long since she felt even faintly sexy. She sees her body, flabby and dimpled, naked against his brown smooth flesh, and embarrassed, passes by the potato salad and loads her plate with low-calorie cucumber, tomato and coriander.

He sits opposite her and spoons lamb curry and roti into his mouth with elegant fingers. His lips curl into a smile. His eyes meet hers, alight with amusement. She feels a frisson of excitement in her nipples.

'Remarkably mild curry for Durban,' he comments, 'Nothing like my wife makes it.'

Her nipples unwind in a backwards spiral of disappointment, her breasts sag, and her double chin doubles again. Bloody hell, she thinks. Typical.

# Addis

There are at least twenty people ahead of her in the queue at visas-on-arrival and it's nearly half an hour before she has paid her $50 and entered Ethiopia. It's a friendly process, more focused on the $50 than on her reasons for being there.

She wanders towards Carousel Four where a handful of forlorn suitcases and a battered cardboard box circulate in slow silence through the almost empty hall. She watches, her tiredness growing with each pass. No olive-green case with a pink ribbon on the handle. Next to her, a middle-aged couple gazes at the carousel with equal concern.

After the same black plastic case passes her for the seventh time, Stella finds a man in uniform. 'My suitcase,' she says. 'It hasn't come through.'

'Boarding pass?'

She hands over the required piece of paper, and after a brief glance, he hands it back.

'Your luggage is going to Mekelle.'

'What?'

'Your luggage is going to Mekelle.' He grabs her boarding pass and points at it.

Her head spins. 'It can't be. I'm only going to Mekelle tomorrow. I need my bag in Addis, tonight.'

'Connecting flight in twenty-four hours, baggage goes to final destination.'

'What?' She wonders if she had too much gin on the plane.

'Connecting flight in twenty-four hours, baggage goes to final destination,' he repeats with deliberation, as if to someone not too bright.

'That's absurd! I need my bag tonight. In Addis. I'm staying in Addis tonight.' This can't be happening, she thinks. Who invented these rules?

'You mean our bags are going to Uganda?' the male half of the worried looking couple interjects in an East Coast American accent. 'We're only going there tomorrow. We need our bags tonight. In Addis. Tonight.'

'Ask that man.' He points at another uniformed man on the far side of the carousel. 'He find your bags.'

This is a very bad movie, thinks Stella, as she hoists her computer bag onto her shoulder and heads off towards 'that man', trailed by the worried Americans.

'My bag?' She holds out her boarding pass to the uniformed bag saviour, who glances at it.

'Mekelle. No problem,' he says as if this were a common occurrence. 'Wait here. I bring.' She breathes a sigh of relief.

The worried man holds out their boarding passes. Bag Saviour shakes his head in a dispirited kind of way. 'Not so easy,' he says. 'Kampala. Big plane. Many bags. I try.'

In two minutes, Stella is handed her rescued bag and heads for the exit, leaving the worried couple in a bagless hiatus behind her. The cool night air hits her as she heads down to the parking lot to grab a taxi to the Monarch hotel.

At the Monarch, Stella is greeted by Ebsituu at reception, and escorted by Ephrem to her favourite room. I'm becoming a creature of habit, Stella thinks, ruefully.

She unzips her bag, hangs her clothes in the cupboard, puts her toiletries out in the bathroom, grabs the gin and tonic from the fridge and settles down on the sofa. *X-men* is the only thing on TV worth watching other than CNN, and she lets it play in the background while she opens her computer. She's watched it before, but it makes a companionable background noise. And Hugh Jackman is in damn good shape for a man of nearly fifty.

She scrolls through her emails and deletes the spam – My Dear, you have been invited to participate in the excellent United Nations conference ... yeah, right.

Delete.

My Dear, my name is Letitia and I was the wife of General Bamajo from Nigeria ... and I am Hugh Jackman's mistress.

Delete.

Best project management training … Delete.

Invitation to an opening of new artists – would be nice, but she'll be out of town.

Delete.

Facebook message, Facebook message …

She scrolls down, deleting, deleting, deleting, and skips any emails that might require her to apply her mind. Facebook message about Afrika Burn. She clicks on it.

A huge T-rex stalks, on fire, through the Tankwa Karoo, brought back to mechanical life in this ancient landscape, a mobile steel sculpture of gigantic proportions. She wonders what fuels the flames as it strides across the desert and sheds glowing coals into the darkness. A photo of Anthea catches her eye – face decorated with sequins, her greying hair windblown, her eyes alight with joy and quite possibly a smidgeon or more of ecstasy. Anthea, maths teacher at Greenside High by day, painter by night, and mistress mojito maker any time of day or night.

There are free spirits, Stella thinks, who launch themselves into life and fly on their own joy and freedom, like Anthea, and then there are those of us who, hoping to fly, find our feet tangled in an old lace nightie, and we fall to our knees hoping no one has noticed our earthbound shame. If they are the free spirits, then perhaps we are the tangled spirits, caught in the mundane debris of our own lives. Not quite brave enough to cast it off and fly.


A temple bell chimes in the darkness. And again. And again. Stella surfaces from a restless dream, swipes off the alarm and stares into the dark room in a vague state of confusion. Where the hell is she and what is she doing today?

As the panic subsides, sense seeps past her puffy eyelids. Addis, she thinks. The Monarch. Arrived late last night. Stakeholder workshop on energy futures for Ethiopian cities. What the hell do I know about energy? Or about Ethiopia for that matter. Another ten minutes, another ten minutes of sleep – I can miss breakfast, grab coffee at the workshop.

An hour later, Stella stumbles two hundred metres down the broken pavement towards the Harmony Hotel where the workshop is to be held. She feels like a bank robber, a fat clutch of birr in worn notes in her bag – transport costs for participants. At least in Ethiopia participants don't get paid to attend a workshop, she thinks. In most other countries she must pay government officials an attendance fee. Bloody international donors, she mutters, I bet they started it.

The workshop venue is long, narrow, and dark. There is no projector. It takes ten minutes to find a hotel employee and even longer for him to return with a projector. Like the room, the projector is tired, her slides a jaded green.

Great, she thinks. Great start.

People start to dribble in, and her Ethiopian colleagues arrive. Stella is relieved to see them – two competent energy specialists, born and bred Ethiopians. She's the strategic thinker here today; they're the techies. She forces herself to wander around the table to greet each person in turn, hearing their names, but not clearly enough to remember them. A couple of government officials, two academics and three people from a research NGO. Only two women, she notes, looking around the table.

Damn, we have a long way to go on this continent before we get to gender equality.

Fifteen minutes late, they start the proceedings. Fifteen minutes isn't bad, she thinks, they're quite prompt in Ethiopia. She launches into her presentation …

Forty-five minutes later the presentations are over and they have broken into two groups – one facilitated by Zelalem, and the other by Stella, who is struggling. Finding a feminist in Isis is easier than getting the participants to talk. Her breakaway group is silent. Six men and one woman gaze into the silence between them as if she isn't there.

She fights down a sense of panic, breathes deeply, and searches for a question that might break the impasse, pushing aside her desire to creep back into her hotel room and watch a crappy police procedural on TV.

Do you guys watch soccer? springs to mind, but it isn't going to take the project forward, and she clamps her teeth shut over the words.

The silence deepens. Grows a little damp and sweaty in the poorly air-conditioned room.

'Technology,' a good-looking man on her left tosses into the silence. 'We need technology. We are doing research on improved cook stoves for *injera*. The people (the women, Stella corrects mentally) don't like to cook injera on electric stoves. It is not tasting the same.'

Stella salivates. She skipped breakfast and took an extra five minutes in the high-tech massage shower instead, easing away her tiredness. Lunch is calling her. She hopes there will be injera, the traditional fermented pancake of Ethiopia made from indigenous teff grass. She loves the slightly sour taste, the elastic feel between her fingers, the decadent pleasure of eating with her hands. She checks her cell phone surreptitiously – still fifteen agonising minutes of silence before they can break for lunch.

She forces a smile into the zombified air and notices that the plastic nametags have Chinese characters on them. Even the name tags? she thinks. Chinese mercantile imperialism at work.

'How much work is being done on renewable energy sources?' she asks, 'Other than hydropower. Like solar or geothermal? Or wind energy?'

Silence.

She waits and wields the silence like a weapon.

'Technology,' the good-looking man intones. 'We are doing research on solar power for heating water. The technology exists. It can be done.'

Still thirteen minutes. Stella summons up her energy like an ancient sorcerer summoning up the dead.

'Are there any plans for renewable energy at any level other than the household? Is the government working on any plans that you know of? Or the private sector?' Silence.

Twelve minutes.

Fuck.

# Mekelle

City of dust and stone, cupped in the rocky palm of surrounding hills. City of battered Toyota Corolla taxis, held together by layers of paint over the rust and dents. City of bone-thin horses pulling ramshackle carts loaded with wooden poles up hills too steep for their fading energy – cart, wood, horse and driver threatening any moment to career downhill in a landslide of dust and flesh.

City of women in white shawls pouring from ancient churches, armed with righteousness against the failure of the rains, the hungry eyes of children, the barren fields.

Stella is overwhelmed by the ancient energy of rock and dust, the stillness of the shrouded women. She feels brash, naïve, a plastic duchess in a world of earth mothers.

It is as if this city, clinging to rock, has stripped her naked, reflected her to herself, so that she sees the hollowness of her life, the empty rhetoric with which she has tried to shape a life of meaning. Has she ever, really, changed anyone's life for the better, or is it all just smoke and mirrors, words blowing in the wind and dust. She is ashamed of how little she has done with her life.

The taxi pulls up at Abnega airport. Stella feels a sense of relief, a drug addict preparing her next fix. An aeroplane awaits – a time capsule of anonymity in which she can shed all shame, all responsibility. For sixty-five minutes, she can be no one. Or anyone. And no one will know. She breathes in the thin oxygen of Mekelle, 7000 feet above sea level. Soon she will be even higher – 24000 feet – and she will survive.

At 24000 feet, she is deep in conversation with an elegant man in the seat next to her.

'The one good thing about the Communist rule,' he says, referring to the twelve years when Ethiopia was run by the Provisional Military Administrative Council, 'is that it was not based on ethnic politics. The leaders came from all over, and it was about Ethiopia, not ethnic groupings. Now,' he adds with sadness, 'now the leaders all come from this Tigray region here, and the resources are all going into this region.'

'And are ethnic tensions building up?'

'Yes, the Oromia majority, who have never been in power, are unhappy about the ethnic bias. It needs to be sorted out, otherwise, there will be problems.'

Stella looks down onto a landscape on which no borders or boundaries are visible. We all have our tribal identities, she thinks. But not all of us go to war because of them.

Stella pulls a nip of gin from the not-cold minibar fridge and reaches for a tin of tonic with the other hand. No ice. No lime. And the only glass is a thick-walled tooth mug, but it promises to be better than the gin and orange juice she had forced down next to the pool the previous night. Orange juice had seemed a fine alternative to the Friendship Bar's lack of tonic, but the sour taste of under-watered oranges clashed with the bitterness of the gin, and she had to sieve it through her teeth so as not to choke on a welter of pips. Not quite what she had been looking forward to.

In the cocoon of her hotel room, with its generic muted lighting, gigantic flat screen, and large white pillows, she pours a stiff herself a stiff drink. Her nose twitches at the surprisingly perfumed tonic as she sinks back into the comfort of the double bed and lets the gin blur the edges of her anxiety. By the time the tumbler is half-empty she stares serenely at an umpteenth re-run of *The Avengers* and tries half-heartedly to remember the name of the actor in the armoured suit, not feeling the usual panic of another name, another word having leached from the interstices of her brain.

By the time the glass is empty, she couldn't care if Loki or the Avengers won. Two gulps into the second glass it becomes even more fuzzy and Loki looks more and more attractive. Oh dear, another sexy bad boy, she thinks. She sinks deeper into the pillows and slides her hand between her legs, feeling her clitoris rise to her touch.

That night she dreams of herself draped in white, playing chorus girl to a bizarre 1980s pop-Loki who sings 'Wake me up before you go-go', in an endless loop that has her fighting the bedclothes to escape the battery of Wham inanity until a door slams in the passage and she wakes into darkness, disorientated and puffy eyed, bedclothes smelling faintly of gin from the spilt dregs of the previous night.

# Dire Dawa

Along the dusty pavements, men in worn trousers and faded shirts slump in cheap plastic chairs, cheeks filled like chipmunks with *khat*, chewing incessantly. Or curl, foetal, in the heat on the flattened remains of cardboard boxes.

Here, between the tall trees and under the hawks that wheel through the dusty sky, the workshop must be over by twelve, in time for lunch and khat, the addictive green leaves of the indigenous *Catha edulis*.

In other cities, men sit on similar pavements on the same coloured plastic chairs, beer bottles or brandy in hand, or pass out, drunk, on hard pavements. But here, Islam rules and available and legal, khat takes the place of alcohol.

'They have no patience here after noon,' her colleague from Addis sneers. 'Even government officials will not go back to the office. They will go home for lunch and to dream and talk with khat. It is very destructive. Everyone only works half a day here.'

Perhaps, thinks Stella, that's how the ragged men on the broken pavements get through the day until it is time to sleep – wrapped in the passing euphoria of that takes them away from their empty-bellied, workless lives, where they scrabble at the margins of this dusty city. Until the effect wears off and they sink into depression and tiredness and crave more.

Women, their heads covered in white scarves, line the street ahead of them. They all face towards an old stone church from which digital prayers emerge. It is Lent, holy fasting month. The women stand and pray amongst the taxis and the three-wheelers and the street stalls that sell plastic buckets, blackspotted mangoes and *bunna*, the strong black traditional Ethiopian coffee.

Stella hopes to learn something interesting during the workshop on renewable energy options, but if not, at least there'll be good coffee. Even in the most remote places, the coffee is good. Unsurprising really, since Arabica coffee originated in the southwestern highlands of Ethiopia. Legend has it that a young goatherd, Kaldi, noticed his goats were excited and wide-awake after eating the leaves of a certain plant and passed on the information to the local monks. They, in turn, made tea from the leaves to keep themselves awake during their devotions. Somewhere down the line, someone seems to have realised that the roasted beans made a much more delicious drink, and the rest, as they say, is history.

The workshop is short, only marginally more productive than the previous one, and over by lunchtime. It is Wednesday, and Stella is delighted to find *shiro*, the local spicy chickpea paste, lentils, collard greens and dark injera available in the hotel dining room.

After lunch, when the participants have headed home to chew khat, Stella and her colleagues take a taxi around the town, her Ethiopian colleagues tourists too in this far-flung town. A bone-dry riverbed cuts a wide swathe through the town, between massive stone walls erected to guide its intermittent flash floods. It is hard to imagine this swathe of sand, baking in the sun, covered in brown, roiling floodwaters.

Later that afternoon, as the plane rises, she sees the huge belt of dry riverbed that slices through the city. As they move away, irregular circles pockmark the land, where hedges corral sheep, goats and skinny cattle against the dry and barren expanse in which they might otherwise wander forever, like biblical figures lost in the wilderness.

The landscape changes – terraced fields cut over centuries into the rugged mountains, taming them for human use. Settlements dot the hills, tin roofs glint in the sunlight.

Here the rivers have cut deep gorges between the heights, and the great tear in the fabric of the earth now below her can only be the Rift Valley.

That night, she nibbles chips and tomato sauce while she meanders across the landscape of Google maps, traversing the Great Rift Valley, and the Afar sunken region where, in a movement slower than time, the continent is tearing itself in two.

She zooms in on the Afar triangle and wonders when the combination of tectonic shifts and sea level rise will flood the barren land with salt water and change the coastline of Africa. Will it happen incrementally, or will it pour in one lazy Sunday morning, filling the Danika depression and giving Ethiopia once again a coastline, lost when Eritrea seceded?

# Easter, Bloody Easter!

It's Easter, four days off in a row, and for once Stella is on the ground, at home, for all four of them, with a bottle of Inverroche Verdant, a stock of tonic, and no plans other than some friends coming round for lunch. It's been a long time since she hosted friends for lunch. The impact of her travels has been a tendency to hibernate when she's home, to dig into her nest and watch the roses slowly unfurl their papish petals.

She scrolls through Facebook, ice-cold gin in hand, feet up on the coffee table, catching up on her friends' lives, the state of the world, and a couple of silly video clips to lift her mood. A gif of an over-excited bald eagle attacking Donald Trump's hair nearly makes her spill her gin. So much for presidential material – even the national bird can't stand being too close to him. Stupid git. And stupid bloody gits who think a man with an orange face and a bad comb-over is fit to rule any nation, let alone one with a red button and a bunch of nukes panting to be let loose.

Bernie now – he's kind of cute and says some pretty clearheaded things. But how did they manage to get a sparrow to land on his podium? Even in America, the land of every weird trained animal, that couldn't have just happened naturally, surely? Birds don't land inches away from some old guy making a speech unless someone told them to.

Stella takes a deep, appreciative sip of Verdant. She might be bloody cynical about politicians – in fact, not much 'might' about it – but she can still appreciate a truly exquisite gin. Not to mention the gentle buzz and the subtle fading away of daily anxiety. Another one or two of these and she might sleep quite well tonight. If only the neighbourhood dogs would stop yapping.

It's not long before she is bored by Facebook. Too many people away for the weekend and the endless anti-Trump rhetoric, funny though some of it may be, is repellent after a while. She turns to Showmax instead, and chooses a documentary on Stonehenge, largely because it isn't one of the screeds of Hollywood series on offer.

What is the rate of OCD amongst archaeologists, she ponders, as a middle-aged woman, grey hair drawn back into a ponytail, explains how it's taken ten years to sort a pile of cremated and crushed bones into sixty-three different bodies. What do you do for a living? I sort bone fragments, day after day, for ten years. Well, that sounds like fun! And what do you do over weekends? Ah, I lie on my back in the garden and look at the clouds as they drift across the sky and dream of being the rabbit on the moon.

Stella chuckles. 'I think I'm now pretty drunk,' she mutters aloud and focuses on the documentary which seems to have moved to Wales where the blue stone for the small uprights at Stonehenge came from. That's not blue, she thinks, it's all bloody grey – why the hell did they choose grey rock from far away instead of grey rock from somewhere much closer. It's all rock after all.

Pony-tailed Professor Archaeology drones on and Stella nods off in her big, soft chair. She drags her eyes open again, to hear the professor talking about some group called the Beaker people, and how things suddenly changed when some guys arrived on the scene with a new technology – metal. Suddenly Stonehenge shifts out of the Stone Age and into the Bronze Age – burial habits change, cultural and social practices change. All because of technology.

And look where that's got us now. North Korea threatening to bomb South Korea if they don't apologise for some alleged misdemeanour; the US using drones to bomb Isis and anyone else who happens to get in the way; a plume of radioactivity in the sea off Fukushima, and the temperature of the world going to hell in a handbasket.

Maybe we would be better off still Stone Age, Stella thinks, sipping Inverroche in meditative mood from a wafer-thin glass. Except that there was no gin in the Stone Age. Or was there?

The next morning the looming lunch drags her out of bed early and into a hand-embroidered apron from a craft project near Thulamela. The lamb needs to sit at room temperature for at least an hour before she cooks it, so she hauls it out of the fridge and onto the counter top, picks up a sharp knife and begins to peel and slice garlic.

Hours later, she is sweating under and over the multicoloured ducks on her apron, but the table on the veranda is laid with an orange and black hand-printed tablecloth from Zimbabwe, her best wine glasses, and pure white plates. A white butterfly orchid glows in the middle of the table, the lamb is in the oven with the roast veggies, the salad is made, thinly sliced nectarine and parmesan nestling on a bed of lettuce, avo and roasted almonds. All ready, she smiles, as she takes a sip of inspirational gin and heads for her bedroom to clean up before the guests arrive.

As always, Lisa is the first to arrive, her internal clock stereotypically precise. As always, she hands Stella a large bunch of roses and a slab of Lindt Intense Orange and kisses her on both cheeks.

'Smells divine,' she says and strides into the room as if onto a stage.

Unfortunate, then, that no one else has arrived yet. Stella places the roses in a Victorian cut glass vase and opens a bottle of Fat Bastard Merlot. The wine gurgles into a long-stemmed rose-red wine glass, and she hands it to Lisa who smiles, smells, and sips.

Nkateko and Richard arrive next, Nkateko, elegant in a tailored African print dress and beaded sandals, Richard tagging along quietly in a checked shirt and chinos. Mark, unsurprisingly, is late, and they are on their third round of drinks when the bell rings, and his tall frame, faded Black Labour/White Guilt t-shirt stretched over a belly that has grown substantially since she saw him last, appears at her gate.

The lamb is a tender, aromatic success, the conversation less so. More Fat Bastard down, and Mark and Nkateko have locked horns in a heated exchange on the benefits and dangers of communism. Annoyed by Mark's wine-inflamed belligerence, there is little Stella can do other than offer more lamb and roast potatoes. Mark helps himself without pausing in a tirade on how misrepresented Castro and the Cuban experiment has been by Western media.

It is Lisa's interjection that stops both Mark and Nkateko. 'As the only person at this table who has lived in a

Communist country, I probably know more about it than either of you.' Mark gapes at her, astonished.

'I grew up in East Germany. I know what it is like.' An expectant hush hangs over the table. ''It was some good, some bad. Like every country. I trained in fine art at the Berlin University of the Arts. My professor was extraordinary …'

Stella, amused, sips her Merlot and watches experience trump polemic. She knows, although Mark and Nkateko don't, that Lisa remains a dedicated socialist, working in Soweto as part of her commitment to social justice through arts.

She turns to Richard, who nurses his beer like an old grudge and watches the others as if from a great distance.

'You still running?' she asks, and his shoulders relax and for the next five minutes, she listens with practised attention to his complex training schedule for the Two Oceans, and his intention to run the Comrades the following year. As he draws breath, she nips through to the kitchen to grab him another beer and retreats again to whip the cream for the pavlova, an exotic concoction that she has never tried before. Not that she made the meringue – that would be a bridge too far. As she discovered, Spar sells meringue shells. All she has to do is fill it with whipped cream and fruit and carry it to the table.

The conversation has moved on. Stella watches with sadness as Mark, now well under the weather, bends Nkateko's ear on the state of the country, his own impoverishment and, wait for it, yes, here it comes, how his bitch of an ex-wife cheated on him and led him into penury. Nearly sixty and still not taking responsibility, thinks Stella.

It was cute when he was a young political science student with sun-bleached curls at varsity in Durban. Less cute now that his abs have vanished under a beer belly and his hair has gone grey and thin. Bloody men, she thinks. Do they ever grow up?

Richard has sunk back into beer-hugging silence, and Lisa toys with her pavlova as if it might bite her.

'You OK?' Stella leans across the table towards Lisa, peering around the Phalaenopsis, which is more annoying than decorative.

'It's my boss,' says Lisa.

'Thomas?'

'Yes. I think he's stealing.'

'From the project?'

'Yes.'

'Oh my god. That's awful. What makes you think that?'

'Petty cash. I handle the petty cash. Some of it's been going missing. For the past few months. And he's the only one who has a key other than me.'

'Oh my god. That's awful,' Stella says again. 'What are you going to do about it?'

'What can I do? He's the boss. I don't want to lose my job.'

And there is the nub of it – office power politics.'

'That's how they get away with it,' Mark butts in. 'All these bloody politicians raping the state. Sticking their hands in the kitty. It's because no one wants to stand up to them … nobody's got any balls any longer. They're all bloody corrupt.'

'Coffee anyone?' asks Stella and ducks into the kitchen. Why the hell did she invite Mark? It always ends up like this; he drinks too much and then he takes on the world.

Aggressively. And with such certainty. It must be so comforting to be right all the time. Bloody idiot. She splashes boiling water on her hand.

Fuck.

Nkateko is at the door, a pile of dirty pudding bowls in her hand. 'You OK?'

'Yeah, fine, just some hot water. Nothing serious.'

'No, I mean you, are you OK? Really OK. You seem sad. What's going on?'

'Sad? Really?' Cynical. Lonely – even amongst friends. Bone-marrow sad. 'No, I'm fine, really. Not sad at all. Maybe just a bit tired.'

'You need to travel less, get some time at home. Rest more. Can I help with the coffee?'

Travel less? Rest more? And let the great emptiness catch up? Stella shakes her head imperceptibly. At jet speed, the emptiness is sometimes left behind. The anonymity of hotel rooms allows her empty soul to rest in peace. For a few nights at least.

'Can you take the plunger through? I'll bring the rest.'

Outside mousebirds scrabble, rodent-like, through the *katjiepiering*, strange feral creatures from another epoch, until they fly, turning modern in the sky, long tails trailing behind them.

# No More Words

The computer screen is deathly still, white bordered by blue, staring at her with cold contempt. Her fingers hover above the keys, hesitant, waiting for the commands to flow from her brain down the nerves, to fire the muscles. The keys wait, expectant, for the fingers to hammer down on them. And they wait. No commands. No nerves that jingle. No muscle fibres that twitch and contract.

In short, nothing happens. She's run out of words. Seventeen pages into the report and there are no more words left. Her brain can no longer muster a coherent sentence. She stares at the computer.

It stares back.

# Abu Dhabi

Stella steps out of the familiar Abu Dhabi airport and into the bone-warping heat of the united desert emirates. She darts into the air-conditioned comfort of a 4x4, which hurtles into the traffic and onto the highway between red, sculpted sand dunes and date palms heavy with dust. Huddles of camels, blonde and brunette, dot the landscape, immobile in the heat. The sky is a uniform grey, the sunlight dissipated.

I've seen this kind of sky in Delhi, she thinks. There, pollution turns it grey. Here it is dust.

It is late afternoon; the sun sinks slowly behind the grey curtain of the sky. Their meetings are over for the day. She is perched on a grey rock above a shoreline fouled with plastic, and a bunch of young Arab men who flaunt their testosterone in swirls and twists on the backs of noisy Jet Skis. They open the throttles, shout and laugh as they compete and grandstand.

Achim and Zara have roared off towards the setting sun on hired Jet Skis, but she has opted to sit, citing the lack of suitable clothes to keep her off what seems to combine the speed and danger of a motorbike with the clutching fear of drowning. She feels safer on her rock, if somewhat dull.

To her right, a bakkie attempts to pull a large boat up a sand slipway. As the bakkie reaches the top of the slipway, the boat just out of the water, all four wheels start to spin and it loses the battle of forwards movement in a spray of sand. Inexorably, the boat sucks the bakkie back towards the water. There is much gesticulation, much shouting, from the men in the boat, the gaggle of men on the shore. More gather to watch and advise. Only the driver of the bakkie, a grey-haired man in a crocheted *kufi* and knee-length white *kurta*, remains silent. He reverses back down the slipway to square one.

A maroon Land Cruiser manoeuvres a Jet Ski trailer through the narrow gap between the bakkie and the edge of the slipway and into the water, the rider perched and ready to accelerate across the water the moment the Jet Ski slides off the trailer.

Stella turns back from watching the Jet Ski hurl itself into the distance like an angry sea-beast to find that the Land Cruiser has been attached to the front of the bakkie and a double towing operation in place – the Land Cruiser towing the bakkie which is towing the boat. Wheels still spinning, the bakkie and its boat are hauled up the slipway, until nose to tail with the parked cars, the Landcruiser is forced to stop. The driver, bow-legged in jeans, t-shirt and mirror sunglasses, jumps out to assess the situation.

After much discussion, they unhitch the Landcruiser, and like Sisyphus, the bakkie descends the hill. Back to square one, except that the tide has gone out a little further, and the boat is less buoyant. Back to square minus one. As the driver of the bakkie attempts once more to pull the reluctant boat from its watery bed, the wheels plough into the sand. The only movement is the bakkie as it sinks into the sand.

Good god, thinks Stella, have these people never driven in sand? They live in a world of sand!

The man in the white kufi has a change of heart and decides that if they can't pull the boat out of the water, they should push it back. With great enthusiasm, he attacks the ropes that tie the boat to the massive trailer, while the boat's motors are lowered into the water. The ropes are stressed too tight to undo, and the man reaches into his pocket for a knife and slices them instead.

The motors roar in reverse and churn the grey water to white foam. But the boat moves not one centimetre.

Stella is enjoying herself. It's like watching a YouTube video in real life. Two men on the boat throw themselves from side to side to rock the boat loose, but it is too big, too stable, and too firmly stuck.

Without a word, the man in the kufi reties the boat to the trailer with what remains of the ropes and climbs, silent and frustrated, into the bakkie. He drives his wheels axle-deep into the sand. Both boat and bakkie are profoundly stuck.

Achmat, purveyor of all things Jet Ski related, smiles at Stella. She shakes her head. 'What are they going to do now?'

'Crane,' says Achmat, with an even bigger smile. 'They bring crane.'

Stella laughs. Good joke. She turns back to watch the Jet Skiers bounce across their own wakes, brake and spin to hurl sheets of spray at each other, and wonders where Zara and Achim are. Out of the corner of her eye, she notices a large truck. She turns, and there, just as Achmat promised, is a bright red crane. Stella snorts. The boring Jet Ski afternoon is turning out to be huge entertainment.

After several minutes of manoeuvring, the bakkie is tied to the back of the crane truck, which moves forwards and pulls both bakkie and boat behind it. Success, almost, except that there is insufficient space for the combined length of crane-bakkie-boat. The crane stops with the bakkie perched precariously at the top of the slipway.

Shorten the bloody tow rope, thinks Stella, but chooses not to get involved in this very male affair in a very foreign culture. Advice from a chubby, middle-aged foreign woman is not likely to go down well.

There is much discussion, again, much repositioning of the crane to pull the boat diagonally where there is more space. Crane, bakkie and boat now form three sides of a triangle. The process is punctuated by the arrival of another 4x4 that insinuates itself between crane and bakkie to deposit another Jet Ski and rider into the grey water.

The crane starts to move forwards.

No, no, no, screams Stella, inside her head. Do none of you have basic physics? This is NOT a good idea.

Doggedly, the crane moves forwards and the ropes between crane, bakkie and immovable boat tighten, and, as Stella predicted, the bakkie is dragged sideways, into line with the boat and the crane, perilously close to the edge of the slipway. Three of its wheels lift off the ground. Excited shouts avert the disaster just in time and the bakkie is lowered back to ground level and slinks downhill, Sisyphean, to its original position.

More repositioning, more shouting, more Jet Skis inserted into the water between boat and bakkie, more repositioning, and at last, a different approach. The crane extends upwards into the grey sky and suspends a metal rod with two ropes on either end over the boat.

Good god, thinks Stella, they're going to lift the boat.

And sure enough, the ropes are tied to the trailer, and as the bakkie strains its way up the sandy slipway, the boat is lifted off the ground to follow the bakkie like a meek sheep returning to the fold. On flat land, the boat is lowered to the ground and unhitched from the crane, and the only remaining challenge is for the silent man in the kufi to edge it, with only millimetres to spare, between the flashy 4x4s and Ferraris parked along the road and out into the traffic.

A Jet Ski pulls up in the shallow water and disgorges Zara onto the beach. Achim follows more sedately behind.

'That was amazing!' says Zara. 'You should have a go. You must be bored just sitting here.' Stella chuckles.

# Kitten

She steps from her car in the parking lot, reaching into the back seat for her bag. It's twilight and light from an open window drifts across the brick pathway. Out of the shadows, a small black kitten skitters over the driveway gravel and brushes against her ankle, tail raised like a radio aerial. She bends down and picks it up, feels its feather-soft fur against her neck, its smooth paw delicate as dawn on her cheek. It gives her a quick cheeky lick that tickles her fingers, twists its tiny body out of her grip and skitters back into the dark. She feels joyful like a little gift has been given to her as she walks towards the anonymity of another hotel in another country.

The scent of dry grass and the vast expanse of the darkening Botswana sky call to her. I must get out into the bush again, she thinks, find a place to sit and listen to the birds. A place where clouds gather over the khaki hills and my lungs fill with the earthy smell of the coming rain. She remembers, in the smell, the promise she made to David. They were hitchhiking to a concert in Swaziland and the storm clouds built cotton-wool castles above the horizon.

'I'll always be your friend. I'll always be there for you. No matter what.' He'd just smiled, dragged on his spliff, and gazed down the empty road where the grass bent in the wind.

# James

Stella is bewildered. She's never shared a house with a troglodyte before and she's not sure how to do it. James has arrived for a two-week stay. He's completed his film diploma and now he hopes to make his way to fame and fortune. Via Stella's spare room.

She's not quite sure how he ended up in her house. Sandra and she don't communicate much. Her sister never forgave her heading off to varsity and leaving her in the middle of the parental cold war.

What a cliché, Stella thinks. Dysfunctional parents create dysfunctional kids who have nothing in common until dysfunctional nephew needs free board and lodging in the big city. He must have something going for him, she muses, he did sweet-talk her into putting him up for a couple of weeks, "Just until I can find somewhere cool to stay, and a job."

It might have been the fact that Sandra wasn't happy about him heading off to Jo'burg that made up her mind. She smiles at the image of Sandra's tweezer lips in Pofadder or Twee-buffels-met-een-skoot-dood-geskiet-fontein or wherever it is that she ended up. Some god-forsaken little Free State *dorp*. With that small-town jock-lawyer husband with a big farm. Fanie. Anglicised, acculturated, ex-Stefanus. With an accent like boerewors and mealie-bread.

So, James has moved into her spare room with his backpack and his worn All-Stars and the cigarettes which he smokes in his room despite her strict no smoking instructions. Her nose twitches every time she gets home.

Her spare room seems to be where he intends to stay. The only time she sees him is when he treks to the fridge in search of sustenance or heads down the road to the café to stock up on B&H – the cheapest brand apparently. Supper, which she imagined might be the two of them at the granite counter in the kitchen, or at the Oregon pine dining room table, chatting about her day and his plans, has morphed into a much lonelier affair than before he arrived.

From the first night, James dished up and vanished, plate in hand, back into his bedroom. She's sure the plates haven't reappeared since, and the hairs on the back of her neck prickle when she thinks of what might be happening to her once neat, white-trimmed spare room, or hears the clink of beer bottles kicked by a casual passing foot on the floor.

What surprises her most is her inability to do anything about it. She has a cave dweller in her space, she hates the music that thumps out from his room, and all she can do is shut her study door, put on a pair of noise-suppressing earphones and listen, somewhat sadly, to the dulcet tones of Mozart's Piano Concerto Number 5.

Sadly, because the presence of another person has made her realise how much she misses intelligent conversation – not the tense conversation of lovers about to part, or the business conversation of people who work together, but the easy conversation of two people comfortable in their own skins. It's been a long time since she experienced that, and she wonders, again, watching her ex-lovers hook up with life partners, breed children and dogs, what it is that has left her so alone.

She even admits, with a twinge of chagrin, that she envies Sandra's relationship with Fanie, envies her this strange boy, closeted in his room. It's too late for her now. She'll be alone to the end – she's sure of that. No charming prince or princess, or ageing king or queen is going to pop out of a pumpkin-coloured sports car and sweep her away into joyful spousehood. Not that there aren't potential kings and queens out there. It's just that she finds it stressful to share her space with anyone. Sharing intimate space is even more so.

The longer she's been alone, the longer she'll be alone. Old dogs and new tricks. So be it. She switches from Mozart to Jimi, searching, perhaps, for a memory of being young, gorgeous and sexually confident.

Who the hell was Mary, thinks Stella, and turns on her computer. One hundred and forty-seven unopened emails threaten to suck her energy into a dark hole. Bugger the emails. They'll still be there tomorrow. She types in "who was mary in the wind cries mary" relieved by no need for caps or accurate spelling even.

Kathy Mary Etchingham. Girlfriend. Jimi took exception to her lumpy mashed potatoes, there was an argument, some plates thrown (by her) and a stormy exit. And a song was born. Mashed potato muse. Strange times.

The web bug kicks in and she pores over pics of Jimi and queries who on earth would call their daughter Lithofayne Pridgon – Foxy Lady's parents it would seem. And whether one could really be born in a place called Dirty Spoon? Only in the US of A! It sounds like a cheap TV show. With the soundtrack by Jimi Hendrix, Afro-American guitar hero with just a dash of Cherokee.

The door opens. The troglodyte has manifested in the flesh and a pair of very dirty jeans, which hang onto the lower edge of his skinny hips by sheer willpower.

She pulls off the headphones and smiles, she hopes in a welcoming fashion. 'Can I help?'

'Hi, Auntie Stella,'

Auntie? No ways. At least it's not *tannie*. 'Hi, James, what do you need?'

'Well, I wondered whether you can, maybe, like, lend me some bucks?'

'Some bucks?'

'Yeah, like, maybe two hundred? Just until my money comes through from Mum?'

She's peeved. This is more than she bargained for. She really doesn't know how to deal with young creatures. Blood relative or not. She twists her face muscles into a smile. 'Yes, of course.' And she reaches for her handbag.

It's 2:13 when he staggers back in, with the clumsy crashing step of too much beer. His door slams and Stella sighs, trying to feel her way back into a dream in which she was curled into the warm embrace of a beautiful woman, high on a mountaintop, the two of them looking out over the landscape in peaceful harmony. But even as she reaches for it, it fades, and she is alone and sleepless in the night.


Interrupted sleep and hay fever – an awesome mix – have turned her eyes puffy and dry. The genius down the passage is still asleep, of course. Breakfast at eleven seems to be his natural rhythm.

And yours, Stella thinks to herself? What is your natural rhythm, trained to order by years of nine-to-five, which is never really nine-to-five but more like eight-to-six, and more, later in the evening? Is this really all it is all about? Five days a week – work. Two days a week – try to relax, fix the house, go shopping, have coffee with friends. And fit in some more work. And then start the five days again. One day she'll be too old and the five days/two days will turn into seven days to potter around the house filling time until the day that the days run out.

This is the purpose of heaven. Not to remove the fear of death, but to offer hope that there is something beyond this daily grind – the grand prize for gritting your teeth and hanging on. But if you don't believe in heaven – or hell? That's when you get dangerously close to suicide, thinks Stella, examining the possibility much as she would an expensive pair of Italian shoes – tempting, but not made to fit her feet. She knows, though, that on dark nights, those shoes may fit uncomfortably well.

What happened to her dreams, she wonders, to her passions and hopes from the days when she too could come home at two in the morning and wake up the next day without needing three cups of coffee and a Panado. What were her ambitions, she wonders, as she stretches back on her memory-foam pillow and stares up at the roof? Aged twenty-something, way back then before the internet and cell phones and driverless cars, what did she want out of life?

To be famous, to make her mark on the world.

For a while, she thought she'd become a famous scientist who found a breakthrough cure for an incurable disease. She was still at school then, filled with fantasies of winning the

Nobel Prize, not the years of research, cooped up in a laboratory with specimens and Petrie dishes and microscopes. Then she wanted to work in film and to write brilliant scripts so that she could meet the man of her desire – some days he was Donald Sutherland, some days Tommy Lee Jones – who would love her and marry her and spend the rest of his life making her feel like Elizabeth Taylor. Nowhere in her dreams was she a consultant, working ten hours a day and wondering what the hell she had done with her life.

She drags herself into the shower and feels the drops rain onto her eyelids and run over her face. She wants them to wash away the bloated eyelids, the lost hopes, the old nightmares, but she knows, as she stands there, that she will step out of the shower with her cellulite and stretchmarks cleaner, her grey hair wet, her jowls needing their daily dose of moisturiser. And she'll grab her computer and her handbag and put on her lipstick and stuff away her ghosts and head off to her office because that's what she does.

She envies the troglodyte his dreams.

# Fig Tree

The soft, fragrant leaves of the young tree brush against her arm as she pats the soil down around its roots. She waters it, admires the terracotta pot and grey-green leaves against the white wall of her back garden. *Ficus carica*, provider of proverbial cover for Eve and Adam's genitals after they ate of the tree of knowledge. Cultivated centuries before wheat and barley – figs dating from about nine thousand years before the birth of Christ were found in Gilgal I, an early Neolithic village.

Which is about five thousand years before god created the world according to the creationists, thinks Stella, as she strokes the soft fur on the leaves. Which makes about as much sense as using fig leaves to cover your most sensitive extremities, since fig sap causes a nasty rash. Was this the world's first hair shirt, or an example of very poor translation from the original?

Figs are also, it would seem, the origin of the Hydra, Crater and Coryus constellations. The ancient Greeks believed that Apollo sent a crow to bring him water from a stream, but the crow saw a fig tree and settled down to wait for the fruit to ripen; a patient crow it would seem, but not too bright. He knew that he was going to get into trouble for taking so long, so he brought Apollo not only water, but also a snake which he blamed for the delay. Apollo, it would seem, unlike the crow, was not patient, and hurled goblet, crow and snake into the sky where they formed the constellations.

Someone in ancient Greece had a vivid imagination, thinks Stella, as the water seeps into the soil. Almost as vivid as those who invented the Garden of Eden and a talking snake. Snakes and figs, she chuckles, is there some connection? And is it true, as Mohammed thought, that figs prevent piles?

She bends over the pot of red geraniums and pulls out a tiny jacaranda tree. They take root everywhere, she thinks. Even amongst the orchids.

# Picket Line

Stella holds up a poster with a mixture of embarrassment and pride. She's on a picket line. She's over fifty and on her first picket line. Mark sent her a Facebook invitation to a protest against presidential corruption, and despite her reservations, she is on a street corner in Sandton with a group of strangers, all holding placards.

Hands off our Treasury.

Support our state institutions.

Down with corruption.

The experience is surprising. She's surprised that she cares enough to have overcome her tendency to sit on the sidelines. She's surprised by the extent of the support they get from the people who drive past, black and white, rich and not so rich. But she is self-conscious. And uncomfortable. Her shoes have small heels and the balls of her feet are tired from holding up her heavy body on the concrete pavement. The sun makes her chubby thighs in her black trousers feel like pork chops on a braai. Her poster has turned soggy where her sweaty hands are clamped to it.

She almost feels part of something bigger than herself. But not quite. The others in the group dotted along the street, clustered on the corners, seem to know each other, to be practised protestors. No one chats to her except to suggest that she move to a busier intersection. She moves, dutifully, accompanied by two other middle-aged women, both in flat shoes, one in a hat.

She is the outsider. Again.

She holds up her poster against the sadness that drags at her chest, and wonders if standing here will change anything. The story of her life. Largely irrelevant. She sighs and holds up her poster a little more aggressively.

# There Is A Face Beneath This Mask

Stella can feel the anger, blue and black, like bruises on her psyche. Deep and difficult anger. Not because of the SMS from a client letting rip about the report she sent last week. Not because a taxi driver cuts in front of them at the stop street and blocks their way while he drops a portly middle-aged woman with two Shoprite packets, a large black handbag, and the mid-afternoon sun glinting on the artificial chestnut brown of her weave. Not because the newspaper billboards highlight another corruption story in government. This is a much deeper rage.

'He tried to poison me,' Desiree, Uber driver of one month, has just said, with extraordinary calmness. 'I wanted to leave and so he tried to poison me. But my youngest drank it instead of me. She died. She was four years old.' No tears, no break in her flat voice. 'I couldn't prove where the poison came from, but I knew it was him. I knew it was me he wanted to kill.'

Stella rages at the men who violate their wives, lovers, children. Attack women in the streets, in bars, on buses. At male power in its ugliest manifestation. At a society so damaged that this violence is committed, commented on, passed over. This morning I got the municipal bill. Last night my husband pulled a clump of my hair out. There's a special on at Pick n Pay. He threatened to kill me if I leave. I have this great new recipe for chakalaka/pears in red wine/*potjie* with kudu. My husband loves it. He loves me too, but he hits me. He broke my jaw so badly I had to have surgery. He bought me a beautiful new sofa from Weatherly's – I'd wanted it for ages. He kicked me in the belly, tore my bladder. They had to stitch it up, but it still hurts when it's full. He didn't like what I'd cooked for supper. He never likes what I cook for supper. My husband hit me with a beer bottle when I tried to stop him molesting my daughter – his stepdaughter. She was seven.

The fury seeps out from a deep gutter and congeals into the shape of Smiley Theron. Stella pushes away the memory and watches Desiree from the corner of her eye, looking to see evidence of pain etched into her face, but she sees only smooth brown skin, a light gloss of lipstick, brown eyes that scan the traffic. She flips down the visor and looks at herself in the mirror, pretending to check her lipstick. She sees the bags under her eyes, the droop of her jowls, the downward turn of the corner of her mouth. Just the signs of ageing she thinks, the pain hidden by the sweep of lipstick, the practised muscle control, the demands of everyday life.

What is it, she thinks, that gives some people an inner glow, a radiation of happiness that wraps around them as they walk through life? Why the hell didn't I get some of that? Because you're a crusty old cow with a cynical view of the human condition and a short temper and none of that leads to a golden bloody aura.

Deep inside, a little girl brushes long-dried mud from her dress and skips across the green lawn. I wasn't always cynical, thinks Stella. Once I had hope and laughter. Once I had dreams. I flew in my dreams, so buoyant that I never touched the ground. I flew through buildings and between the tall trees of ancient forests, I flew over lakes and over the yellow and red sand of huge deserts. Like an angel, I flew above the world.

Haven't done that for a while, she thinks. Now I dream of narrow passageways in dark buildings where rats scratch at piles of unidentifiable rubbish and I must squeeze and twist, unable to see the way out. I walk between bombed-out buildings and stub my toes on fallen chunks of concrete in the half dark, my suitcase heavy in my hand, my way unclear.

'Here we are.' Desiree's voice cuts into her reverie and Stella half sighs, half chuckles. Enough self-pity, she thinks and swings her legs out of the car, scrabbling for her keys to the sound of Seven Avengfold or Doomslayers or whoever they are, thumping from her spare room. Three weeks and the troglodyte shows no sign of imminent departure. She opens the gate and Desiree drives away into the traffic with the ghost of her dead child.

Stella steps through her front door into a wall of sound and the faint smell of smoke and tears rise in the back of her throat and tickle her nose. Her sanctuary has been colonised. By a creature from a different landscape. She feels adrift. Untethered. She floats, jellyfish-like, into the kitchen and opens the fridge. No tonic. She opens the drinks cupboard above the sink. An empty gin bottle mocks her, a sentinel in a wooden cave. She drops it into the bin. Hears it clunk against the bottom. Dried tomato sauce leers at her from a jumble of once-white plates in the sink.

She grabs her keys and flees, leaving the invading army ignorant even of her coming and going. She drives directionless – anywhere, but not here. She twists and turns down the narrow Melville streets, through the busy movement of couples and groups of friends, squeezes past double-parked cars and the uncertain gait of drunks, onto the calm of Carlow Street, and right into Westcliffe Drive. The bar at the Four Seasons will be open. Gin and tonic with a view of the city. Anonymity amongst people.

Much later, cocooned in a fluffy white dressing gown, she lies back against the overstuffed pillows on the king-size hotel bed and laughs. A sad, amused, post-coital snort, like a quiet hyena with hiccoughs. Armand? Was that his name? Remarkably sexy for a balding man with a paunch. French accent. French fingers. She still tingles. She reaches for the glass beside the bed but it is empty, so she reaches for the phone.

Room service? A double Inverroche Amber with ice and lime.

What attracted him to her? Was a gin-drinking woman on her own easy prey for a man away from home looking for a quick bit of sex? Or did he really find her attractive? Middle-aged, middlingly fat, middlingly grey Stella? She can't visualise herself as attractive any longer. It's as if that part of her life has drifted away on the currents of time, and she is surprised that anyone would want to make love to her.

Make love, she thinks, what a misnomer. Have sex with her, in a rented room in a hotel, the night before he left for Ouagadougou. Probably a bloody arms dealer, she thinks. He didn't talk about his work. Neither of them talked very much. And now her laughter is clear and refreshing. What the hell, she thinks, who cares what he thought. It was a long time since she'd orgasmed at the behest of someone else's fingers. Thanks, troglodyte, she smiles, your dirty plates and my night of illicit sex. She rolls over into the pillows and snuggles into the clean white linen.

# Delhi

The three of them stumble off the plane and into the immigration hall, Stella with some trepidation. Last time she was here, the hall was a wall to wall press of humanity; the start and end of any one queue indistinguishable in the squeeze, while seismic waves marked the spots where opportunistic queue jumpers found a vulnerable traveller and forced their way past, often in groups of seven or eight, generally men.

Tonight it is weirdly empty and it is only a matter of minutes before they are through and headed for the luggage belt, where the trouble starts.

The thousands that were in the arrivals hall last time she was here are now concentrated in the baggage hall. Achim and Saul grab their bags from the carousel and step back into the mêlée, leaving Stella to stare at the carousel for what seems to be hours, willing her familiar battered case to arrive; but it seems neither her willpower nor her suitcase has made the journey with her. Minutes add to minutes and still no suitcase. Beside her, fellow travellers lift off their overstuffed bags, their shiny hard-shell cases, their boxes tied with coloured twine. And still she waits. And Achim and Saul wait for her.

'Dubai this side,' an official-looking woman in orange explains to a frustrated passenger. Stella glances around, confused. From what she can make out some of the bags from Dubai have been unloaded from the carousel and lined up haphazardly on the near side of the carousel. On the other side stands a wandering line of bags from Doha.

Anxiety gnaws at the edges of her tired mind. How is she to watch the bags on the carousel and look through a growing line of bags in the throng of bodies that are milling – well, just milling.

She's trapped, unwilling to give up her ringside position at the carousel, yet concerned that her bag might be lurking in the crazy line of luggage on the other side of the carousel. She looks to Achim and Saul for assistance, but they have vanished into the ocean of people grabbing for bags and space. After five minutes of paralysed tension, her case, tiny between the excesses of other people's travelling needs, appears.

Relieved, the three of them head for gate five where their taxi driver and the foul air of the world's most polluted city await.

At four in the morning, the Delhi roads are relatively empty, making it easier to see how local drivers play out the decorative curves of Indian art and architecture. No one drives in a straight line. Everyone weaves and winds, with no apparent reason other than the pleasure of not being trapped by the tyranny of the white lines. She tries to relax into the weird lane-changing dance of their driver on the empty road, closing her eyes and breathing deeply.

But there are mosquitoes inside the car, and by the time they pass under the first "foot-over bridge" as the green sign labels it, her sandaled feet and ankles are measled with bites.

As she scratches her feet against each other in an agony of itch, they overtake trucks with once-decorative cloths, now dark with exhaust fumes, hanging behind them, a rickety cart drawn by an emaciated nag, and cardboard and plastic hovels that cling to the pavements like limpets exposed by the tide.

The Pampoen Hotel (formally the Pamposh) has a high-tech lift with touchscreen buttons. But the touchscreen has retired itself and the lift from active service, and she must drag her body and suitcase up to the first floor where her room appears to be as close to the railway line as is possible without actually being under the wheels of the passing trains.

She crawls into bed and tries to ignore the vibration of the trains through her cranium, only to be bitten by some unknown assailant, annoyingly close to the as yet unhealed three-in-a-row bed bug bites from the hotel in Addis. She scratches the bite and her itching feet twist and rub compulsively against each other.

Gradually she begins to unwind and yawn and sleep beckons, only to be snatched away on the back of a goods train heading for Hyderabad. She rolls onto her side and tries to meditate.

Breathe in two three four, hold two three four out two three four five six. Feel your body, feel where it touches the bed, feel any discomfort – like my bloody itching feet – and let it go let it go. Do not hold the thoughts. Let them rise up and go … please, can the bloody trains rise up and go!

At last, sleep overtakes her, to be interrupted only too soon by the chime of a temple bell. She turns the alarm off. Waking up short on sleep, in the wrong time zone, to the gentle sound of a temple bell, doesn't make her any happier than waking to the sound of a goods train that roars past. She slides from the bed and staggers to the shower. The cold shower, hot water having gone the same way as the touchpad in the elevator. She showers briefly, scrubs the cold away with a tired towel, and pulls on a pair of black trousers and a synthetic, crease-proof shirt. Hair dried into some kind of style, a smear of lipstick and she is ready for the day. Or as ready as she is going to be.

# Death

The chime of an electronic temple bell rings her out of the second night of trains. She pries open her eyelids and wonders, half asleep, where she is. Her eyes search in the faint light that seeps through the curtains for something familiar against which to anchor herself and find only her open suitcase, spilling clothes lazily onto a bed next to her.

Slowly the fog of sleep recedes. India, she remembers. Delhi. Pampoen Hotel, with the fancy lifts that don't work, and the noise of passing trains. She turns on the light and reaches for her iPad. She has twenty minutes before she must get up. Twenty minutes to check emails and Facebook.

When life deals you lemons, crack out the tequila, is Stella's general view. Or the gin. But when the lemon is blasted at you at internet speed in the half-light of a foreign dawn, not even tequila is enough.

Anthea is dead.

Beautiful, vibrant, whacky Anthea is dead.

Stella rereads the messages and stares at the photo of Anthea at Afrika Burn, posted on Facebook by a grieving friend. She hopes this is a dream, struggles to believe the words she reads. Anthea is dead. Knocked off her bike on her way to work. Stella stares at Anthea's radiant smile in the vast expanse of the Tankwa Karoo, remembers David's wry smile, feels the sting of every unfair loss in the back of her throat.

Rage and sorrow spin inside her skull, like a *warrelwind* across drought-stricken fields. Spinning and spinning they hurl dust and dead mealie leaves against the back of her eyes, filling them with tears that flood down her crumpled cheeks.

No. No. No. Rage against the futility. She screws her eyes shut but the dust devil whirls more wildly and blasts against her cranium, sandblasts her heart.

Inside the mini-fridge, a nip of gin, ice-cold tonic. She raises the chipped tooth glass to towards the ceiling. Cheers Anthea, she says, up there, out there, wherever you are, if you are anywhere now. I'm going to miss you. Dreadfully. Cheers, David. The bitter-sweetness slides down her throat and dampens the dust devil which slows and teeters. But the tears still fall.

Anthea, who had been painting obsessively for a solo exhibition after years of friends persuading her to believe in how good she was. September, in the Red Room in Rosebank. Ten canvases. Last time Stella saw her she had been working on number eight – a grey, brown and pink abstract inspired by the dust roads and rose quartz rocks of Namibia. It was a remarkable piece that captured the essence of an ancient landscape, the arid smell, the insignificance of the watcher in that desolate place.

Stella had wanted to buy it, but Anthea had laughed and told her she'd have to wait. 'You made me do this exhibition,' Anthea smiled, 'so now you can wait until they are all up and if you still like it, you can have it.'

Oh, Anthea, I'd rather have you back than any painting of yours. Stella wipes her face on the white sheet. Time to put on her big-girl pants and face the day. She has a presentation to give. It's an international conference and they've paid to get her here – she can't let them down. She swings her feet to the floor and stands up. Her heels are sore where the tendons attach to the calcaneus. It always takes a couple of minutes for them to loosen up. She hobbles towards the shower like an old Chinese woman on bound feet. Shit, she thinks, I hate getting old. Your body starts cracking up, and too many people you know are dead. What a shit world. If there is a god, she sure as hell didn't think through the details of her grand vision.

Despite the prompt delivery of a hairdryer and an iron by room service, Stella feels both fluffy and flabby as she smiles at the young woman behind the registration table and hopes that her eyes aren't too red from crying.

'Mrs Bellamy.' The young woman smiles and hands her the conference pack – on recycled paper with a paper nametag – no plastic here. Stella is too fragile to correct the woman, accepting by default her married status.

Men in suits and Indian waistcoats swarm around her, their density leavened by flashes of silk – butterfly women in saris and salwar-kameez, confident in the exquisite dress of their homeland. Stella pats at her hair, hoping it hasn't frizzed too much in the Delhi humidity. She sidles into the conference room, trying to locate a plug to keep her computer alive for the day, a lifeline for her electronic addiction.

The Minister of Energy is due to open the conference, and so, of course, they wait. And wait. Stella is used to waiting for the lords and ladies of state. Once, a lifetime ago, she was a civil, or perhaps in her case. An uncivil servant.

So, she does what she always does – opens her computer and buries herself in emails and Facebook where the accolades and tears pour in for Anthea. Stella remembers when they met at Mark's fiftieth. So few years, thinks Stella, and yet it is as if you have been part of my life forever. Until now. What am I to do without your whacky generosity to counter my grumpiness? Just as the lump in her throat is about to choke her, a butterfly woman takes the stage – a fearsome if slightly battered moth, perhaps. Her silk is dark in hue, her hair greying, her intelligent eyes rove the audience as she explains her role as head of one of the subcontinent's most powerful NGOs.

How she's aged, thinks Stella. How we have all aged. Except Anthea. Anthea will never age, caught in the permanent brightness of early death.

An inveterate multi-tasker, she half listens to the opening remarks, half engrossed in emails, despite the knowledge that multitasking results in two tasks done badly. Disjointed phrases catch her attention: energy poverty, energy justice. This is not her world, the energy world – she's here as a water expert, but the phrases resonate: energy justice, social justice, water justice. Phrases of courage and integrity. For all her cynicism, she feels at home here, with people who want to change the world. It's what she would like to do, although in her case it is probably more words than reality.

Stella wonders if she had never existed, whether the world would be any different. She sighs and deletes an email announcing that she has won the UK lottery. Yeah, right, she thinks, 4.7 million pounds. Like hell I should be so lucky.

The day is long, and by the time it is Stella's turn to present, they are an hour behind schedule, it is after five, and she can feel the lethargy in the room. She tries hard, perhaps too hard, but the audience is lost, their minds on the traffic, or what's for dinner, or just nowhere at all, and she feels an edge of panic. This is what she's good at, presenting, telling the story of water, communicating with audiences of all sorts and types. But she knows she hasn't reached them. She is gutted. She has let herself and the organisers down.

She came all this way, at their expense, for a ten-minute presentation no one was interested in?

By the time the other three speakers have finished, there isn't even time for questions. Another group has booked the venue for the evening and they are hustled out in undignified haste. Today is not a day that Stella is going to remember with enthusiasm. She heads to her bedroom and hopes for an ice-cold gin and something on TV that will take her mind away from death and mediocre presentations.

# Indira Gandhi International

# Airport

The man at the baggage X-ray machine demands to see the luggage tag for her computer bag.

'They didn't give me one.'

'Get one. Over there.' With a vague gesture towards the teeming departures hall.

'Where?'

'A baggage tag,' interjects a youngster next to her in the baggage queue, enunciating carefully for her benefit.

'I'm not stupid,' she snaps. 'I speak English.'

He shrinks, picks up his bag, and melts into the crowd. As she stands there, stupid after all, a second guard produces a spare baggage tag from his pocket, ties it to her computer case, stamps it, and sends her on her way amongst the passengers and buy-me-buy-me duty-free shops.

Great, she thinks, not even eight o'clock and already I've ruined some poor kid's day. Why am I so fucking grumpy? What is the magic switch that will make me kind and caring and serene? Delightful. Full of delight.

It feels like a long time since she was filled with delight. She tried a gratitude journal in the hope that it would bring back a sense of delight. But it became just another task and she pushed it to the back burner and forgot about it.

She avoids the music that thumps from the Delhi Daredevils Sports Bar and settles into Starbucks with an iced hibiscus tea, *Stella* scrawled across the disposable cup as if to make the throwaway moment more personal. And for a moment, when the young man behind the counter called her name, it almost felt personal. But it was too practised. Like birthday wishes from the optician, and the dentist. We have programmed our machines to show we care. Yeah, right!

Over her iced tea, she watches two young women and an older man, each at their own table, deep in conversation together about their travel experiences. Peru, Bali, India. She wonders who initiated the conversation and why, wonders where each one is headed, where they have come from. The blonde on the left rises, summoned by the announcement of flight EK623, boarding at gate A23. The atomic bonds broken, the other two rise, proffer awkward goodbyes, and drift into the crowds like free electrons, strangers again.

At the next table, sit two couples, one American, one German. Stella, eavesdropping without shame, deduces they've been with an international youth tour to India. A litany of moans litters their conversation about 'the kids of today' and their music. 'They don't even buy albums anymore,' the Yank pontificates. 'They just download singles illegally and share them. They don't even know who they're listening too.'

Not the youngsters I know, thinks Stella, or the one I know, as she remembers James, head sunk into his hoodie, educating her about Trivium and Sevenfold Avenge, with an encyclopaedic knowledge of their music, their best tracks, their band history. She wonders how he is doing. She hasn't heard from him since he moved out, and she misses him. Not that she's contacted him either.

The conversation at the neighbouring table has moved onto cyber paranoia and apps with built-in Trojans that roam your device collecting data and transmitting it back.

Back to whom, wonders Stella? Big brother? Big brother's rather nastier criminal cousin? Or big brother business which tracks your every move to send you targeted adverts to get you to buy more. And more and more. Oh bloody hell, Stella thinks. Who cares? I can always delete their emails.

# Making Contact

On the pavement outside the Lucky Bean, Stella slouches in a low armchair, sips orange and cinnamon tea, and grapples with a tsunami of emails. A tiny girl, elfin curls wrapping her face, approaches with the simple curiosity of the very small. Stella smiles at her, and the creature edges closer, dark eyes barely blinking, like Bambi in the woods. Stella smiles again. Hides her eyes behind her hand. Peekaboo. The tiny face lights up. Little hands cover her own eyes and peek slyly from behind splayed fingers. Stella hides again. The little girl edges closer.

The big round eyes fixate on Stella's earrings and she sidles nearer as if drawn by a powerful magnet. She points.

'Earrings,' says Stella and wiggles her head a little so that the Ethiopian amber swings against her neck.

'Eewigs.' The word is so newly minted that it slides not quite formed off the little tongue. '*Gogga*,' she says, pointing to the chair, or so Stella thinks, but it could have been something else.

'Mm,' smiles Stella. 'Gogga. Under the chair?'

'Unda tcheh' mimics the elf and tastes the words like she might a new flavour of jelly.

'Yes,' says Stella, 'gogga under the chair.' She tickles her fingers across the little girl's head, who giggles with the innocence of the very young. Stella smiles. This is so much more fun than emails.

# Caught

On either side of the N1, laser-levelled fields stretch brown and barren towards the horizon. A warrelwind picks up dust and leaves and hurls them into the air. The tar shimmers in the heat, raising illusions of water in front of the car. Outside the temperature is 35°C. Inside, the air conditioning blasts cold air onto Stella's feet and chest. It is the fourth year of drought and no mealies have been planted. The land is parched and topsoil hangs in the air in a fine cinnamon dust.

The sky stretches from horizon to horizon in a bleak and relentless blue that drains the energy from Stella as she drives. She feels desiccated. A mummy behind the wheel. She's on her way to Bloemhof to pay a traffic fine. Under new legislation, more than thirty kilometres per hour over the speed limit requires a court appearance, and so she's on a six-hour round trip to make her first court appearance ever. She's nervous.

The Bloemhof traffic department is in a freshly painted building with a row of red geraniums blooming on the pavement. A short, middle-aged woman with carefully curled hair and pink fingernails greets her, turns her around and ushers her out, pointing to the courthouse down the road.

The courthouse is surrounded by neatly mown lawns. In the entrance corridor, a row of people wait on wooden benches and Stella, uncertain of what to do, joins them.

As they wait, they begin to chat. The young man next to her is a student, and to her dismay, he has brought a lawyer with him to fight his speeding charge.

Do *I* need a lawyer, Stella wonders with a hint of panic?

'I can't afford to lose my licence,' he says.

I can lose my licence? Stella is now panic-stricken. What am I in for here? I thought I was just going to pay a fine!

Inside the court, they sit on more wooden benches. And wait.

The magistrate is an unassuming man with a touch of grey in his hair, black-rimmed glasses and a dark blue tie. As he sits, the prosecutor stands and introduces the first case. The magistrate remands a dishevelled young man in a dirty t-shirt and torn jeans to a later date. In the second case, the magistrate reads the riot act to a scrawny man with bloodshot eyes and bad skin – he has clearly had in his court before.

'You have to stop this, do you hear me? You cannot go near her again. You must leave her alone. You know this. I don't want to see you here again.'

The man nods in submission, is remanded, and shuffles out. It sounds to Stella like a repeated domestic matter and she hopes there wasn't violence involved. She's embarrassed that the judicial system must waste time on her speeding fine and wonders how the magistrate copes with seeing these broken people back in his court time and time again.

'Martin Ackerman,' calls the prosecutor. The student takes the stand while his lawyer moves to a table in front of the magistrate. Stella is glad the lawyer is there. He talks his client through the charge, what he did, his remorse.

I can copy that, thinks Stella.

'What do you do?' asks the magistrate once Martin has confessed to having broken the speed limit, admitted that he is sorry, and moved from the confession box to the sentencing box, which seems to be different for some arcane reason.

'I'm doing my PhD at Wits.'

'On what?'

How is this relevant, thinks Stella?

'On whether students from rich households have a stronger voice in presenting their side in arguments than students from poor households.'

'You're getting a PhD in that?' The magistrate can't hide his amused disdain. Stella snorts with laughter and stifles it before she is faced with contempt of court. 'Just ask the students from the Tshwane University of Technology!'

'I'm sorry, sir?' Martin flounders, bewildered. His lawyer is silent – this is not his field of expertise either.

'The students at TUT have been fighting about fee increases for years. No one listened. Who are they – just a bunch of poor black kids. The rich white universities, UCT and Wits, join in and now everyone is listening. Seems to me that your PhD is self-evident. How much can you afford?'

'I have five hundred Rands, sir.' Martin looks chastened on many levels. 'If it is more than that I'll have to ask my parents.'

'Then I'll fine you five hundred Rands,' the magistrate smiles. 'Any more than that, I would be fining your parents, and that wouldn't be fair.'

'Thank you, sir,' stammers Martin, and ducks out of the box.

Then it is Stella's turn, and, after she confesses that she was a bad girl and is very, very sorry, and after she has moved to the sentencing box, the magistrate asks what she does.

'I'm a consultant in the water sector.'

'Ha!' says the magistrate, 'Can you fix our water problems?'

Ouch. She knows the problems here – five babies dead from contaminated water, major interruptions in supply due to water shortages, only partly due to drought. Not a single engineer working for the municipality. And an insufficient budget to fix the problems.

'Um,' she says.

'Never mind.' His smile is frayed around the edges. 'How much money do you have? A thousand Rands sounds appropriate.'

'Yes, sir.' Stella breathes a sigh of relief. She'd expected it to be more.

'Pieter Smit,' calls the prosecutor.

She leaves the court to pay her penance and drive the three hours back to Johannesburg, amused, and yet chastened. And from deep in the past, her mother's voice comes back to her, 'You don't want to end up in jail, Stella, do you?' Jesus! What was that about?

She is just outside Potch when the memory surfaces. She was about twelve, in her last year of junior school, and she'd come back from the doctor with a *Tessa* and *Kid Colt* photo story. She'd been halfway through it when the nurse called her to see the doctor. She'd wanted to read it to the end, and she knew her mother would never let her buy it. Her mother despised photo stories. So Stella asked for it, and old Dr Lennon had laughed and said she could have it, with pleasure. Her mother found her on her bed, poring over it. Stella remembers her mother's dual horror – that she was reading such trash, and that she must have stolen it.

'But Dr Lennon said I could have it, Mum.'

'I've spoken to you before about telling the truth.'

'I am telling the truth, Mum.'

'Don't lie to me, Stella. You know what happens to people who lie. You don't want to end up in jail, do you? You must take it back and apologise.'

'But Dr Lennon said —'

'You heard me, Stella.'

Why don't you believe me, Mother?

After school the next day they drove to Dr Lennon's office. Sandra the Good smirked in the front seat. The elderly receptionist had looked confused and embarrassed.

Stella still remembers the bitter taste of the false apology. Yeah, Mum, she thinks, it took nearly fifty years, but I ended up in court after all. But not yet in jail.

# Litunga of the Lozi

The small plane lifts them over the vast expanse of the Kafue National Park to Mongu in Zambia's Western Province. Stella, soaking up the landscape through the small window, wishes she were at ground level, driving through the thick forest, over the rivers and between the hills. It is untamed land below, and it calls deep into her soul.

From Mongu, it is half an hour in a 4x4 with failing air conditioning before they reach Lealui, and the residence of the Litunga, keeper of the earth, representative of the god Nyambe, and King of the Lozi. It is the dry season, so the Litunga is at his palace in Lealui, in the floodplain of the great Zambesi River.

They arrive at the unostentatious palace where the Prime Minister and his team of all-male flunkeys greet them in the dusty parking area. Stella is curious and tries to stifle her annoyance: to enter the palace and meet the Litunga, the men may enter from the car park, while the women must go all the way around to the other side of the compound.

It feels like the back entrance, and Stella's vaguely feminist leanings are not impressed. The culturally respectful and PC part of her, on the other hand, recognises that this is not her world or her culture, and so she follows the guide obediently, stopping every so often at his instruction to crouch and clap to announce their arrival. Her knees are growing sore from the crouching and standing by the time they enter the large, square hall.

A row of white plastic chairs stands in the middle of the hall, facing the empty throne. They are ushered to the chairs and asked to wait. She sits, nervous about not offending, while a group of elderly men wander in and sit on the floor on either side of the hall. The Prime Minister, fly whisk in hand, enters, and takes up his position on the floor closest to the throne.

And they wait.

After a long silence, the Litunga, a mild-looking man with glasses and an elegant midnight blue suit, enters and takes the throne. Stella smiles – she expected more pomp, more circumstance, someone less modern.

The Prime Minister addresses the Litunga in siLozi. Since there is no translator, Stella can only imagine what he might be saying – My Lord, here's another bunch of so-called development experts who want to meet you – they don't seem to be offering much in the way of money, but they might have some good ideas. If you can just hear them out and take a photograph, they'll go. Or it could be a traditional praise poem to the strengths and weaknesses of the Litunga, spoken in ceremonial Siluyana.

It could be anything. She is way out of her depth.

The seated men speak in unison, a short phrase, and clap their hands. The Prime Minister speaks. The seated men speak in unison again, the same short phrase, and clap their hands. Stella wonders if she should be clapping but chooses stillness as a safer option. There are no women for her to copy and she's wary of stepping into the morass of gender roles.

The agricultural specialist from the Netherlands in the chair next to her shifts uncomfortably, his two-metre frame incompatible with the sequential constrictions of a small plane, the back seat of a 4x4, and a lightweight plastic chair.

The Prime Minister turns and welcomes them on behalf of the Litunga, and at least this part is in English. Jaap van Doorn, leader of the team, still seated, as is required, addresses the Prime Minister – no one speaks directly to the Litunga. He introduces them, explains their visit, their project to improve agricultural productivity in the floodplain. Speaks at length about the importance of the floodplain and his respect for the Barotse people.

At last, the Litunga speaks. He speaks in well-honed English, directly to them. He welcomes them and wishes them well in their endeavours, speaks of the importance of development in his kingdom, of how poor his people are, of how they were coerced into becoming part of Zambia by the British. He speaks of the promises of development, the lure of the copper mines, the looting of Barotse coffers by the Zambian government. His voice grows stronger as he speaks of the lack of investment in Barotseland by the Zambian government, how they have been discriminated against, how they wish to become an independent nation.

Stella is startled. She wasn't expecting a statement of intended secession. She wonders how Jaap is going to handle that one.

But a dialogue is not intended. The Litunga has spoken, and there is no debate. The Prime Minister speaks again, in siLozi, and it is all over bar the photographs. Jaap is invited to sit next to the Litunga, and while the cameras are positioned, the right angle sought, the two sink into deep conversation.

Stella is paralysed. She'd love to talk to the Litunga, but she is one of the only two women in the room, and unaware of what taboos she might or might not break. Mind you, she thinks, this nation was originally founded by Queen Mwambwa, wife of Nyambe. She handed over the throne to her daughter, Queen Mbuywamwambwa, who, for some reason lost in the mists of history, handed over the throne to the first of the male Litungas, and no queen has ruled since then. There are not many queens left in Africa.

In South Africa, thinks Stella, the Balobedu in Limpopo are ruled by a queen, the Modjadji, with an inverted gender history to that of the Litunga. As far as she can remember, the Balobedu broke away from the Monomotapa kingdom in south-eastern Zimbabwe after the king's daughter, Dzugundini, fell pregnant with her brother's child.

In a place and time where incest was punishable by death, getting far away must have seemed like a good idea. Her mother, legend has it, stole some rainmaking charms – ostrich beads, red and blue beads, and a piece of an assegai – so that her daughter and her followers would be blessed with rain wherever they went.

Where they went was south, to the misty mountains of what is now called Modjadjiskloof. Dzugundini's son, Makalipe, born around 1600, became the first of six male rulers of the Balobedu. The fifth king, Keale, annoyed by some of his older sons' sexual interest in some of his younger wives, ruled that the throne would not automatically go to the oldest son but rather, according to the approval of the ancestors.

A hut was built in the royal *kraal* when he died, and whoever could open the hut, male or female, had the approval of the ancestors and would become the next ruler. Keale's son became the next king, but he was so unimpressed by his sons threatening to kill each other that he secretly trained his daughter, Modjadji, in the rainmaking rituals. He died in 1800, and she opened the hut.

Since then, the Balobedu have been ruled by women, all called Modjadji. However, remembers Stella, in recent years there were some surprising deaths of queens in quick succession and the remaining heir apparent is too young to rule. And so, for the first time in 200 years, a man rules the Balobedu as regent. The previous queen, muses Stella, the first one with a good education, died at the age of twenty-seven, variously from AIDS, meningitis, or poison, depending on who one listens to. As someone who liked wearing the latest fashions and hanging out in nightclubs, being confined to her kraal and having to speak to outsiders through a male representative must have been tough.

Another cultural conundrum thinks Stella. Modernity and tradition make for strange bedfellows.

In the fields outside the palace, unkempt canals cut through the floodplain, cattle dot the green, and women carry enamel basins of fish on their heads towards a waiting truck. The harvested fish of the great Zambezi flash silver in the midday sun. The occupants of the truck lounge on the scrubby grass, waiting for the women. Plastic packets of ice line the truck, while empty packets, their frozen contents melted away, festoon the fields like tired condoms.

Without haste, the women lower the basins from their heads onto the ground, the truck men gather round, and the haggling starts. These are not the world-renowned razor toothed tiger fish or the giant *vundu* catfish, but the smaller yellow-bellied bream, and tilapia with three shadowy spots marking their silver flanks. As Stella and her team wander away to look at the canals, blotched with sand and weeds, the men load the fish into crates in the truck and pack them with ice.

Stella wonders where they are heading for, and how much the women were paid for their catch. Little enough, she imagines. They have little power of negotiation out here and few options other than to sell to the men with their trucks and their packets of ice. An empty packet somersaults past in a sudden breeze, and Stella sighs. She turns to look at the fish pond where farming tilapia adds to the income of the woman who tills this piece of land – part of their research project here.

That night, in the tawdry hotel, with dusty African drums in the foyer and mosquitoes in the courtyard, Stella nurses a lukewarm gin and tonic alone in her bedroom, avoiding both the mosquitoes and the rest of the team. She's had enough of company for the day. She needs not to have to smile and nod. She needs to sit still after the bumpy flight and the rocking of the van over bad roads. She hopes the gin will ease the residual feeling of nausea, although ice would make it easier. The icemaker, it seems, has given up the battle against the heat, laid down its sword, and retreated into the land of broken technology.

Stella gazes at her bare feet and thinks about the women carrying loads of fish on their heads for long kilometres in the hot sun. She remembers the all-male court of the Litunga. God, the privilege of being white and middle class, she thinks.

# Epiphany

Stella has an epiphany. A strange thing to happen standing over a pan of scrambled eggs, ignoring the sink full of yesterday's dishes, but it's her experience that enlightenment happens more often amongst the dirty dishes than in a shaft of light descending from the heavens accompanied by the far-off sound of violins.

She's bored. Deep down in the marrow of her bones, she is bored, with getting up and going to the office and sitting behind her computer thinking and writing, or sitting at home thinking and writing, washing dishes, calling an artisan to fix the electrical or technical entropy that grips the house from time to time. Bored with her self-repeating circle of friends. With the ongoing cycle of diets that never work. Bored even with watching *Game of Thrones* to avoid being bored.

Bored with being bored.

What the hell does one do at nearly sixty when you are bored with your life, she wonders, scraping the eggs from the non-stick pan onto a white plate and sprinkling them with pink Himalayan mountain salt. Bored with bloody scrambled eggs even, she thinks, scraping them off the white plate into the shiny Italian steel rubbish bin. Bored with white plates, she thinks, tossing the plate into the bin with the eggs.

How does one un-bore a life?

Many years ago, she met a woman in the dining room of a hotel in Delhi. They were both alone in a dining room packed with eager-eyed computer techies gathered for a three-day conference. The woman, elegant in a green and red silk sari asked to share Stella's table. Stella, not so grumpy in those days, smiled and nodded. Prof Akhalwaya was a professor of English at Delhi University, specialising, if Stella remembers correctly, in post-modern Indian literature. Whatever postmodern Indian literature might be. For six months of the year, at least. The other six months of the year, she spent as a nurse's aide in a remote village in Bihar, administering vaccinations and basic medical treatment.

It seemed to Stella at the time to be a remarkably balanced way to spend one's life, but somehow she never managed to implement anything like it, even on a small scale. Perhaps she's too selfish? And besides, what skills does she have to offer someone in a poor rural village?

*Get some skills*, snaps the devil on her shoulder. Not so hard to do.

'I don't speak the languages of rural people in South Africa,' she argues.

*Then work in the city where people speak English*, sneers the devil, a banner saying 'soup kitchen' hanging against the dingy wall behind him.

'I've tried,' mutters Stella, 'I Googled a whole lot of charities to find somewhere to donate my time, but I couldn't find anywhere that called to me.'

*Called to you?* The devil is beyond sneering now, well into the next level of contempt. *You think this is a calling? Like Mother Theresa, or Desmond Tutu? The only thing calling to you*

'I didn't mean it like that. It just didn't seem there was anywhere that I would feel comfortable and that would fit with my work demands. My travelling schedule. All the stuff with kids needs you to be there on a regular basis. Half these places are run by devout Christians and they're going to look at me oddly within half an hour of me getting there. One "fuck" and I'll be iced out of the door.'

*So don't say fuck.*

'You know what I mean.' Stella brushes the devil off her shoulder and there is a faint scrabbling, not unlike the scritchings of a cockroach, as the devil searches for her dignity amidst fluff and dust dogs behind the sofa.

*Oh, Stella, she calls out, you know something – the back of this sofa is a metaphor for your life. Look a little behind the surface and you'll find the dirt.*

'Oh, fuck off.'


So, she does it. She takes a step to avoid boredom. She decides to do something new every month, and the first step is skydiving. Tandem skydiving admittedly, but diving through the soft blue of the sky nonetheless.

On Sunday morning, she pulls on a pair of white jeans and a blue t-shirt, hoping that it is appropriate gear for jumping out of a plane. It's horribly early for her on a Sunday, but she's packed a light lunch – avo and cheese on health bread with a bottle of Sir Juice pomegranate – and she's ready to go. She's checked the tyres and filled up with petrol, and now she just has to find the place.

An hour later, she pulls onto a dirt road to the Rustenburg Flying Club, gripping the steering wheel to hide the slight tremor in her hands. The place is a hive of activity, and she wanders across to join the line of people as they sign away their rights in order to jump.

I will not hold Rustenburg Flying Club or any of its members … she reads, and signs without bothering to read the rest.

Chances are, she thinks, if anything goes wrong, I won't be around to sue anyone. The thought makes her smile, but her signature is oddly uncertain on the page.

In the large hangar, two men fold parachutes carefully and methodically. She hopes they got a good night's sleep, hopes they know what they're doing. One of those contraptions of thin fabric and long strings might be the one that keeps her from hitting the ground at terminal velocity.

The instructor measures her middle-aged body with his eyes.

Not the slightest flicker of lust, Stella notes with sadness. There was a time when a man like him would have measured her up and down more than once. Now it is a cursory glance and he hands her a set of red overalls to put on.

She steps into the overalls, zips them up, and sits down on a bench to wait.

And wait.

It is a slow process. There are only two tandem divers, and six people signed up to jump with them. She is number five. So, she waits. No book, no internet. Just the sun and the wind and a battered silver plane touching down and taking off. And coloured 'chutes that blossom in the sky and fall slowly, ever so slowly, to ground. Until they're close to the ground, when they seem to Stella to fall frighteningly fast. More than once, she wonders why she is doing this. But she's paid her not inconsiderable fee, and she's determined to jump.

Quite why she is so determined to jump eludes her. She always swore that she'd never jump out of a plane. Bloody stupid idea, she's always thought. And yet ennui has brought her to this place.

She knows she'll be terrified, as she watches a young woman climb into the plane for a tandem jump, surrounded by eager solo parachutists. Oh my god, she thinks, heart thumping against her ribs like a large trapped frog, it's going to be awful.

She watches the plane rise into the cloudless sky, smaller and smaller, until one by one, blue, red, white, green, the parachutes burst from its flank and begin their slow descent.

She watches the tandem dive, wondering what it will feel like. The dive looks wrong somehow, lumbering through the air, not drifting like dandelion seed. She watches with growing concern.

Is it meant to look like this? It seems off course, wounded. They're coming down fast and they're too close to the fence. Why is he so close to the fence? The two of them, tied together with webbing hit the ground heavily, roll, and for a moment, lie still.

Stella stares in shock as slowly the two of them get to their feet. The trainer helps the young woman to her feet, holds her arm as she walks. What the hell happened? Stella feels a surge of adrenaline hit the pit of her stomach.

'She passed out!' The trainer looks pale as he babbles to a colleague. 'We jumped, and she passed out. Like jumping with a bloody sack of potatoes. I've never had that happen. Thirty years and no one has ever passed out on me. I heard about one guy who had a heart attack, but I've never had anyone pass out on me before.'

'You next?' He stares at Stella who blushes at being caught eavesdropping.

She nods. 'I think so.'

'Just don't pass out!'

'I'll try not to.' She smiles, but he's not in a smiling mood. He turns away to check the packing of his parachute.

Half an hour later, it's her turn. Without ceremony, she is thrust into a somewhat undignified harness, yanked tight by Oscar, her tandem partner. Then she is bundled into the plane amidst a group of young men, each with a parachute strapped to his back. Before she knows it, she is seated on the floor of the plane between Oscar's thighs, and he has clipped webbing straps from her harness to his.

They taxi down the runway and she waits for the adrenaline to kick in, the terror to strike. But she finds herself curiously calm as she watches the young men run through a series of strange, personal rituals. One touches each of his fingers against his thumbs, twice. One appears to pray. Their rituals are more disconcerting than the idea of being strapped to a strange man and about to throw herself out of a plane.

She remembers just how dangerous this sport is. But still no fear. Perhaps her fear centre has shut down in the face of her stupidity.

'We pull the cord at this height,' Oscar breaks into her train of thought. She looks out of the window, still calm.

I'm going to shit myself when they open the door, she thinks.

And then Oscar pulls her up onto his lap and tightens the straps so that she is bound to his chest in an intimate embrace. He checks each of the straps. Tells her to put on her goggles. Reminds her how to jump, how to curve her body back when they are in free fall. She feels the anticipation, waits for the door to open, the terror to hit.

Instantly the door is open and there is no time for fear. She hangs in the air, a monstrous wind buffeting her. She feels motionless in time and space, just the violence of the wind reminding her that she is plummeting to the earth at terminal velocity.

Her body is arched back, head up, arms and legs up, and she is a dolphin in the waves, a glass of wine in coq au vin, chocolate sauce on vanilla ice cream. She laughs and her lips flaps in the turbulence. She is a Valkyrie of the air.

Oscar pulls the ripcord and with a painful yank of the harness on her crotch she is upright, the noise has gone and she drifts like dandelion seed above the world, looking around in meditation and delight.

Far too soon, the ground is close below them.

'Pick up your legs,' Oscar reminds her, and they slide, almost gracefully, onto the ground. His arms slips around her in a hug. 'Thanks,' he smiles, and she beams back.

She is in love. In love with Oscar, with the sky, with the ground, with herself. The club photographer snaps her smile for posterity and she walks, ten centimetres above the ground, back to the hangar to return her harness and her red overall and to collect her photos.

'That,' she thinks to herself, 'was not boring!'

In the car, she must hang onto the steering wheel so as not to drift away like a dandelion seed, through the open window and out into the vast blue of the cloudless sky.

# Office Politics

Stella is battling to keep her eyes open. They're on item four on the agenda, Office Logistics, and Sarah and Zara are arguing about whether to have red or orange chairs in the lunch room and what style they should be. Stella really couldn't care less. She couldn't care less about most of the stuff on the agenda. But every two weeks she dutifully sits through the arguments.

Last time it was what biscuits to buy. The time before it was whose job it was to clean the cups from meetings. The time before that, it was something else equally petty. Do these people not have real issues to worry about?

Her mind swings to her presentation for tomorrow's workshop. She turns her agenda over and begins to map out the slides.

# The Man at the Gate

The dregs of society have washed up against her gate. The man's voice is so thin and shaken by tears that she struggles to hear his story. She's sure he says his name is Samantha, and with his high-pitched voice, she almost believes it might be, except that he seems to be talking about a daughter. She's heard his story before, almost word for word, from other dregs that float on the tide past her door.

'Tannie, I've been thrown out of the place where I was staying, me and my daughter. I swear we've been sleeping in the park for the last three nights. Last night, three black men came and started messing with me.' The tears pour down his face and he wipes his nose with a grimy fist. He is pathetic.

'Luckily a white man came along and saved me. I've found a place where I can stay. It's called the Mercy Shelter, but the problem is, tannie, that I have to pay them forty Rands a month.'

'Forty Rands?' She is absurdly relieved. She expected him to ask for a couple of hundred at least. Forty Rands is easy. She turns away to fetch the cash.

'Tannie, does tannie maybe have an old blanket as well?'

'I'm not sure. I'll look.'

Her purse is nearly empty – she is one Rand short. Not a spare coin to be found in the house. And not an old blanket either. She drags an old curtain from the cupboard. It is fairly thick and no doubt better than nothing. Winter is coming on and it will shield him somewhat against the cold.

'*Dankie*, tannie, thank you so much.' For thirty-nine Rands and an old curtain. Tears run down his cheeks again. She is embarrassed by how little she has given.

She goes back into her warm house and her cold gin.

# Fish River

The winter morning air carries little needles of ice that prick and startle in the pink lining of Stella's lungs, sting her eyeballs like sand. She is at the bottom of a 650 million-year-old desert canyon, clad in thermal underwear, thick socks, a fleece beanie, and despite the fourteen kilograms of backpack, she feels antlike.

It's day three of the hike, and Stella's thighs are beginning to recover from the agony of the never-ending descent into the bowels of the earth. By the time they reached the bottom of the canyon on day one, she cursed having agreed to come on this hike and wondered whether her legs would carry her as far as the soft beach where they were to camp that evening, let alone another ninety kilometres.

The next morning she could barely stand, and only heavy doses of Myprodol enabled her to clamber over boulders that seemed to get bigger and more hostile at every turn and plod through soft and treacherous sand that robbed her legs of energy, staring at the golden walls of the ravine as if it were an evil force determined to kill her.

At night, while the others chatted and sipped lukewarm whisky, she crawled into her sleeping bag and waited for the Myprodol to ease her muscles into submission. Even the tracks of a leopard across their campsite couldn't keep her awake.

Take me out of this agony, she pleaded silently to the spotted predator. End it now. But he kept his distance, a ghost in the night.

If she'd known what it would be like, she'd be ensconced in her faux Gommagomma armchair, sipping ice-cold Inverroche and reading Barbara Kingsolver, not slogging her way across an endless expanse of rock and sand.

Serves you right, she thinks, as she digs her stick in so as not to overbalance on the smooth rocks.

Agreeing to other people's dreams.

'I've always wanted to hike the Fish,' Nkateko had said. 'They say it is absolutely amazing, a really spiritual experience.'

And Stella had allowed herself to be talked into it. Had even bought a new ergonomically-designed backpack for the trip – which squeaked every time she took a step. If it didn't have her food, her sleeping bag and her painkillers in it, she'd throw it into the river right now. If one could call it a river. At times, it is barely a metre wide, the water-worn rocks, exposed by the drought, shimmering like dry pearls in the midday sun. She fumbles in her pocket for an energy bar and stumbles forwards.

Halfway, she thinks, we must be halfway. If I made it this far then I can make it to the end. I think. I must. No other way out.

Nkateko and Richard are patient with her slowness. They settle onto rocks and breathe in the silence while they wait for her to catch up. Patrick has a different technique. He vanishes like a mountain goat to explore nooks and crannies, to swim, to take photographs, bounding over rocks as if his backpack was filled with helium.

Stella's backpack is filled with lead. The *tokoloshes* are loading it with extra lead every night while she sleeps. Her knees are sore, her back is sore, and she can't see what is spiritual about slogging your way through nearly a hundred kilometres of rock and sand with a heavy weight on your back and not even a hot shower to relieve the hell.

At least the suppers are good. Nkateko and Richard have catered superbly, and by the third evening she is able to take part in preparing supper, to appreciate the couscous with almonds and dried apricots, and to chat by the light of an almost full moon before climbing into her sleeping bag and sliding into deep sleep despite the discomfort of the rock mattress.

It is the last evening, though, that catches her unawares. They are camped next to the river, on rocks worn smooth by centuries of water. She is tired, but most of the pain has gone. Or she has become used to it.

Above them the setting sun paints the cliffs with gold, warming the hostile rock into statuesque beauty. A full moon rises in the darkness, bathing them with light so clear that they turn off their torches.

With a slight smile of surprise, Stella realises that she is content. Nothing matters other than being here, under a numinous moon, in this vast and silent canyon. Maybe that's what they mean by a spiritual experience, she thinks. Being at one with the world. Sounds corny, but it feels good.

# The Dragon's Lair

She feels untethered as she speeds through the air in a metal cylinder, ten kilometres above the ground. Below, strange peaks and valleys, scoured by wind and long-lost rivers, lie bleached by the sun. They fly across what must be millions of square kilometres of sand, decorated with faint runes of habitation and roads that make no sense amongst the bleakness.

Why would anyone lay out fields in this sand, surrounded by desert? Larger patches of tilled sand appear, not connected to the two dead straight ribbons of tar that run across the landscape of beige and grey. A larger settlement passes below them. Thousands must live here, she wonders, in neat rows against the sand. No colour breaks the monotony. Is it oil, she ponders, that has drawn them here, or water, deep beneath the sand, that nurtures something under shade cloth. What do they grow here, she contemplates, and why? And where the hell am I, anyway? Kashan, she sees on the map on her screen. Bobol.

Good lord, she thinks. I'm over Iran. Closest I've ever been to the Ayatollah. And to think that this was all part of Africa before it drifted away and smacked into Asia. That's what those mountains were, she thinks, the folded mountain belt of Iran. Amazing!

Then all signs of people vanish. All that is left is the bones of the earth laid bare by wind and time, the meandering paths of ancient rivers, knife-sharp peaks of sand and rock, in a pallet coloured by geology. Ferrous red, granite grey, pale brown, salt white. In places, they swirl and blur together as if deposited in oxbow lakes and wide, slow rivers, or tortured into beauty by tectonic powers. It is hard to imagine this country once fertile with water and vegetation.

And above the white-cloud horizon, an unutterably blue sky.

Then a greater surprise – incongruous in the barren landscape, a sudden peak, whitewashed with snow. Volcanic in origin, millions of years old. Mount Damavand, where the mythical Persian king Freydun chained the three-headed archdemon dragon, Azi Dahaka to wait for the end of the world. He chose not to kill him so as to prevent him, rather unpleasantly, bleeding vile insects and venomous snakes into the world in his death throes.

She can't see any dragon's breath in the cold air, and she wonders, whimsically, if the end of the world has come and gone, or where the dragon will go when the world ends? And what does the end of the world look like? Will we go out with a nuclear bang, or with the sad whimper of another species going extinct? What will happen to the people in planes, the day the world ends – will they take off in the normal chaos of the modern world and land, one flight later, in the apocalypse?

# Chocolate Lesbians

The scrawny young man in the seat opposite her, eyes glued to his cell phone, thumbs working overtime, is wearing a gooseshit-green shirt that states: 'Cover me in chocolate and throw me to the lesbians'.

What the hell does that mean thinks Stella? That lesbians will eat anything that's covered in chocolate, even heterosexual men? Was he given the t-shirt, which might make wearing it excusable, or did he see it in a shop, think it was witty, clever, sexy, and pay for it himself? Idiot.

And then, because clearly it will be a while before their flight is called and since she can, she Googles it: origin of cover me in chocolate and throw me to the lesbians.

It is variously attributed to Jerry Springer, The Opera (which turns out to be an opera based on the Jerry Springer show written by Richard Thomas and Stewart Lee), an anonymous UK band called the Chocolate Lesbians (how can a band with a name be anonymous?), Garth Ennis (who's he?), and a volunteer at the West Coast Women's Festival sometime in the 70s. Some say it's an expression of surprise, along the lines of 'Well paint me red and call me Sally', some think it's a sexual fantasy that needs no detailing. None of which explain why the scrawny young man scratching his ear in the seat opposite has it emblazoned across his chest or what he thinks it means.

Stella shifts in her seat, annoyed by the delayed flight. As usual.

Paint me red and call me Sally, or Jane, or Stella, or butter my butt and call me a biscuit, and any peculiar forms of expression in between appear to be common to southerners in the USA, according to one Daniel Sosnoski, who claims to be a professional editor with more than twenty years' experience, currently specialising in medical publications.

Why is a medical editor writing about strange American sayings? Slap my ass and call me Clementine. Tickle my anus and call me Samantha. Really? Well drill my teeth and call me Jaws.

Stella flips to her emails instead, scrolling through them without really looking.

# City Birds

Every city has its signature birds. In Nairobi, it's the marabou storks, shades of dirty old men in shabby black jackets and off-white shirts that gather, oversized, in trees, on rooftops, on rubbish dumps, watching and scavenging. In London, it's sparrows in literature, and feral pigeons in reality. In Durban, flocks of Indian mynahs screech in the jacarandas – alien birds in alien trees.

In Colombo, on the new highway in from the airport, pelicans perch on the lampposts, watching over the traffic like large-billed gods and goddesses. In the centre of town, where cement and corrugated iron shops lean tiredly against each other, book-ended by the glass and chrome of prosperity, it is hordes of grey-headed crows that spawn in the trees along the electricity lines that snake from pole to pole, the red-painted roofs, and the tops of walls. They fill the sky with myriad dark shapes, rats of the air, squawking and squabbling, never still. As ubiquitous as the tuk-tuks that weave and bob through the traffic.

The Hilton Hotel has an unimpressive entrance. It springs on her out of building sites, badly tarred roads and swarms of tuk-tuks, but it is cool and clean inside, and they take her case and offer her a glass of ice-cold, freshly squeezed lemon with sugar. Delightful refreshment against the crippling humidity of the outside world. She feels her shoulders relax, her lips settle into a smile across her furry teeth that scream for a brush after the long flight.

As she steps into the lift, a man steps in behind her. They smile at each other across the trapped space with that familiar yet distant greeting of two people in a lift. He's younger than her, clad in a suit, tie slightly loosened, short hair. Businessman, she thinks. Out from Europe to discuss business.

'You look lovely,' he says, and she is too surprised to identify his accent, to place him in the world.

'Thank you,' she smiles, embarrassed, and he smiles back as he steps out on the fifth floor.

She continues upwards. Was he hitting on her? Did he really think she looked lovely? Or did he see a lonely middle-aged woman desperate for kindness? What the hell, she thought, no idea what that was about, but I'll choose to think he really did think I look lovely.

She steps into her room and stops in front of the full-length mirror. Nice shirt, she admits to herself, looking at the huge flower in shades of turquoise on a silky black background. Nice haircut too, she admits, looking at the professional impact of Verashnie on her increasingly grey locks. A once pretty face hiding amongst the jowls. She smiles at herself.

What a sweet man, she thinks. Now if I can get a gin from room service, all will be wonderful.

Just then, outside her window, a pile-driver starts a heavy-metal rhythm that thumps into the ground and rattles steel against steel. *Gaddumph clunk. Gaddumph clunk clunk. Gaddumph.*

Oh my god! She stares out of the window as if her glance

alone could freeze the steel into stillness. How long is this going to go on for? Better make it a double gin!

Around the houses below her, the crows have been replaced by giant bats, the so-called Indian flying foxes. If the crows called up shades of du Maurier, this is pure Nosferatu. The size of ducks, the bats swoop and flap between the silhouettes of trees sewing together the light that spills from street lamps, shops and the open windows of homes, silent against the shuddering thump of the piledriver.

She remembers the pale face of Nosferatu in the 1922 silent movie as he rises, rigid, from his coffin, and wonders who determined that if two people of illegitimate birth gave birth to an illegitimate child, that child would be a vampire, and wonders even more why her brain should have retained that peculiar piece of information.

My brain needs a defrag, she thinks.

A ring at the door heralds a man, not a vampire, in a black and white uniform, who carries a plate of her favourite cashew nut and pea curry, and an ice-cold gin and tonic. Thank heavens she's staying in a Western hotel where alcohol is available despite the strictures of Poya day, the Sri Lankan version of Uposatha, the Buddhist celebration of the full moon.

Poya is a day of fasting, and it being December, this Poya day is the day of Unduvap which celebrates the arrival of the Bo Tree sapling in Sri Lanka from India. It was brought by Theri Sanghamitta, daughter of the Emperor Asoka and his first wife, Devi, and founder of an order of Buddhist nuns in Sri Lanka.

Devi, she reads on Wikipedia, daughter of a merchant, didn't accompany Asoka when he became Emperor, and their two children became committed Buddhists, not royalty.

There's a story there, thinks Stella, Googling further – Asoka and Devi and the ascent to power.

Instead, he married Asandhimitra, princess of a small kingdom north of what is now the sprawling, polluted metropolis of Delhi. She was his chief queen for thirty years, and Asoka lost the plot after her death, like so many older men, marrying her young maid. The early version of running off with the secretary thinks Stella with disgust, and she sips her gin and turns away from the sexual vagaries of ageing men and back to the Bo Tree.

To Stella's amusement, Wikipedia describes the Bo Tree as 'the right-wing branch (southern branch) from the historical Sri Maha Bodhi at Buddha Gaya in India, under which the Lord Buddha attained Enlightenment.'. It's not the idea of attaining enlightenment that makes her chuckle – that sounds like an excellent idea, but a right-wing branch? Not unlike the special branch under apartheid? What would a left-wing branch look like? Would it have a red flag draped over its twigs? Would it be severed from the main tree with a sickle, and be hammered into the ground?

Apparently, she reads further on, the right-wing Bo Tree is the oldest documented tree planted anywhere in the world, having been planted in 288 BC in the grounds of the monastery at Anuradhapura.

That's a long time ago.

Bugger the tree she thinks and slumps back into the sofa, gin in hand. She reaches for the TV remote and wonders what will be on offer other than the ubiquitous CNN. She has no desire to watch CNN. The Americans have elected an orange-faced, xenophobic sexist, with the brainpower of a crow and a lot less compassion. She has no wish to see his pursed pink lips spewing his peculiar brand of petulant hostility.

Democracy is a deeply flawed system, she thinks, sucking on her gin. It might be the best we have, but it's pretty bloody awful.

She channel hops, skips over CNN, Bollywood movies, Sri Lankan news and endless programmes of chanting, yoga and meditation.

She pauses for a moment as a woman with a strong American twang explains how they inherited a dog from a beer-drinking friend. 'When he left tawn,' she drawls, 'he gave his dawg to us. It was a reely sweet dawg. He called it Heineken and the name kinda stuck. We tried to change it, but he only came if we called him Heineken. So it kinda stuck. So after he's been with us a coupla weeks, the dawg, I mean, we're in church on Sunday. We go to the evangelical church. We been members there a while now. My little wun, she's only three, and she falls asleep on my lap in the service. It's a kinda long service that day 'cause its Easter, and the preacher, he's gowin' on a bit. So she falls asleep on my lap. Just when the preacher asks us to pray, and it's all silent in the church, ma littl' un, she wakes up, and she says, kinda loud, "I want my Heineken!" Well, b'lieve you me, I had to do some 'splaining to the preacher 'bout that one!'

Stella chuckles and flips to the next channel and the next and the next, skips the cricket and the next cricket and the soccer, hoping for a decent movie or series that will take her mind out of the trials and tribulations of her life and the world for an hour or two, at least.

*Rush Hour 2*. Good god, no.

*Twilight*? Vampires disguised as pale-faced, pretty, young things? Perhaps appropriate with the bats outside, but no.

She reaches for her meeting notes. Tomorrow she will meet the Secretary of Irrigation and Drainage. They want assistance in revising their water law – and she's head of the team they have pulled together to assist.

She puts aside the meeting notes. She's been over them already – there's not much more she can do in preparation. She opens Google maps and zooms in on the Anuradhapura Sacred City. She'll be there in a couple of days, and she wants to see it from the air before she ground-truths it on foot. Sure enough, she can clearly see the Jethawaranamaya Dagoba, the circle of the cupola set into a square base, and around it, the precise outlines of ancient buildings, over two thousand years old. It fascinates her to see from the air how it was set out, how many sacred sites litter the modern city. She zooms in and clicks on the little yellow figure that allows her a street view, but all she manages to find are roads lined with bushes. Somehow, she can't get to see the sacred sites from the ground. She seems to be trapped on the same piece of empty road going first one way, then another.

Bugger.

She searches for Sigiriya instead, and a massif rises from a bed of forest, the square lines of human habitation strange against the rounded treetops. The garden area is edged, at least on one side, by a moat. She Googles it.

The massif is the remains of a two-billion-year-old magma plug from a volcano that once spewed molten lava onto the plains around it. Now, after aeons of erosion, all that remains is the hardened core, rising sheer-sided from the plains. With a palace on top.

Some fifteen hundred years ago, Prince Kashyapa, son of the king and a commoner, had a bit of a dalliance with his cousin. His father, the king, unhappy with this, killed the prince's mother by boiling her alive – the sins of the son visited on the mother. Prince Kashyapa, equally unhappy, walled his father, the king, into a dam wall and took over the throne. His half-brother, son of the king's royal wife, fled to South India, and, according to myth, Kashyapa, scared that his brother would return with an army, built a fortress on top of a massive chunk of rock, two hundred metres high.

On Google maps Stella can see the layout of the rooms, the water storage tanks carved deep into the rock. The entire top of the massif is covered with ruins. Some stories indicate that the king had started to build the palace before his unfortunate death in a dam wall, which makes sense considering that, according to Wikipedia, the wicked prince didn't get to live in his fortress palace long enough to have built its complex and beautiful structures. His righteously pissed-off half-brother, Moggallana, returned from India about twenty years later, conquered Kashyapa and moved the capital back to Anuradhapura. According to legend, in his last act of defiance, the commoner prince slit his own throat, raised his dagger in the air, and fell over dead on the battlefield.

Moggallana turned Sigiriya into a Buddhist monastery. She wonders what the monks made of the pleasure palace of the dead prince with its paintings of naked women on the walls.

CSI Miami rolls across the TV and her attention switches from ancient family squabbles to the brutal murder of a prostitute in downtown Miami. Murder and violence, she thinks, a particularly human trait. Not pretty.

After five stressful hours of competing with tuk-tuks, garishly decorated trucks and buses, motorcycles, bicycles and stray dogs, her driver pulls up in the parking lot of Sigiriya. Her meetings over, she has given herself three days to tour Sri Lanka in a hired car with a driver. She has no desire to negotiate Sri Lankan traffic, where the art seems to be to avoid eye contact with other drivers as you force your way into the perpetually moving mass of traffic.

Ticket purchased, she walks through the torrid, moist air trapped between dark green trees, towards the entrance to the gardens and the fortress palace. She crosses the moat and walks up the central path. On either side lie the remnants of elegant gardens, dotted with water features where, even now, fifteen hundred years later, water bubbles up under natural pressure through carved stone fountains. The decorative engineering fascinates her, and she is amused by the description of this place as a fortress. This garden was designed for pleasure, not war.

She walks on and up, towards the towering massif from which the wicked prince surveyed the world around him. To get to it she passes through a narrow passage between two huge boulders. A metal sign nailed to one of them warns her to be quiet lest angry hornets attack. The warning picture is both graphic and cartoonish. She smiles and squeezes through in silence.

A metal staircase takes visitors halfway up the front cliff to a cave in which the prince's harem has been immortalised on the wall. She wonders how the painter got this far up a cliff without the benefit of a metal staircase, as she stares in fascination at the pomegranate breasts of semi-naked women, the exquisite face of a clearly African beauty. She's far from home, she muses.

To the north, the famous Lion Gate marks the entrance to the palace. According to the pamphlet she picked up, you can see the head of the lion in the cliff face behind the gates. She gazes at the feet of the lion that hug the gate, sculpted from the mother rock fifteen centuries before, and sweeps her gaze upwards to look for its head in the brown and grey granite above them.

No lion's head that she can see. She looks back at the feet and starts to chortle. To someone who has seen a lot of lions' feet, has even held a lion cub on her lap, these are not lion paws. Lions do not have three claws, turned inwards. They have rounded paws with four claws. She matches them against a memory database of images. She's seen animal feet like this before.

Tortoises, she realises. These aren't lions' paws, they're tortoise feet.

Her eyes sweep the cliff again and sure as nuts, there is the head of a tortoise, turned sideways, a round cave forming its eye.

She starts to laugh. This isn't Lion Gate. It's Tortoise Gate.

As she stands in the hot sun, in front of the ancient gates, while tourists stream past her, out of sheer curiosity she Googles tortoises, Hinduism and Sri Lanka. To her astonishment, she comes across an article which explains that

Kasyapa means tortoise and that Prajapati, chief god of the Brahmanic age, took the form of a tortoise to create the world. Later, Vishnu took the form of a tortoise to rescue various items lost in the great deluge. He also, as a tortoise, supported the world.

Surely, she thinks, she can't be the only person to make the link between the feet at the gate, the head in the cliff, tortoises, Kasyapa of Hindu mythology and Prince Kashyapa?

Other references refer to a large lion sculpture through which the stairs used to go. But she much prefers her own interpretation. Hello, Tortoise Gate, she smiles and walks through to begin the long climb up the metal staircase to Kashyapa's folly on top.

Sweaty and out of breath, she steps onto the top of the tortoise. The view is spectacular – three-hundred-and-sixty degrees over the forest. In the distance, a white Buddha rises through the dark green canopy. Below her, the delicate order of the ancient gardens is visible.

A paranoid playboy, she thinks. He saw this place and went, 'I want to live *there*. Up there.' And because he was a king he made it happen.

How many commoners died building this place, she thinks. They had to build a staircase up the side of a two hundred-metre cliff. It must have been absurdly dangerous for those who constructed it. But it must have been remarkable – she'd love to see a reconstruction of how they made it possible for a king to walk on air to his palace in the clouds.

She imagines the people who served him as they staggered up the long staircase loaded with meat and vegetables, up and down, up and down. It must have been hell, she thinks, worse than the steep, narrow servants' staircase in the double-storey houses of wealthy Victorians.

Bloody hell, she thinks, the ordinary people have a rough time around the rich. She gazes at what must have been a swimming pool carved deep into the granite. Definitely a playboy, she thinks. And not one who cared too much about his people, despite his commoner origins. Or perhaps because of his commoner origins.

She is reminded of the Taj Mahal, of her naïve surprise that such an exquisite and expensive building served only to house two corpses. The folly of the rich and powerful, she thinks. Happy to sink the economy as long as they get to live out their fantasies. Maybe all kings have more than a touch of narcissistic personality disorder, she thinks. Or at least those who have made their mark on history.

In her eco-hotel that evening, she showers off the heat and sweat of the day, too ashamed of her cellulite-ridden thighs to expose herself in the blue temptation of the swimming pool. She hasn't owned a swimming costume for a couple of years now. She collapses onto the bed and orders fish curry and gin from room service rather than sit alone in the dining room amongst the happy chatter of the other residents. She switches on the TV and hops in a desultory fashion from one channel to the next, while she feels the cool air-conditioned air sweep over her body.

She's tired, and her eyes are already closing by the time the fish curry knocks on her door. Spoon in one hand, she opens a new page on her laptop and starts to type.

Tomorrow is Anuradhapura, she thinks. At least it's flat. No bloody stairs to climb, and no murdered fathers, boiled mothers, or megalomaniac monsters making their indelible mark on the landscape.

Her thighs have set into hard blocks of pain, and the hot, sticky air dissolves both her composure and her hairstyle as she steps out of her room.

Bloody hell, she thinks, why am I doing this?

She climbs into the car, yawns, and they move off into the tuk-tuks, buses, trucks, taxis and their accompanying fumes. Even an elephant. It is an hour and a bit to Anuradhapura, ancient capital of Sri Lanka for a thousand years, modern traffic willing. She leans back and closes her eyes, thankful for the endless patience of her driver, Kalinga.

At Anuradhapura, she steps out of her air-conditioned cocoon into the sweltering humidity. She feels the internal prickles start, triggered by heat, a moment of bone-bending exhaustion, and a hot flush that runs through her body leaving her red-faced and even more sweaty.

'Bloody menopause,' she mutters. 'Does it never go away? How long do I have to live with this torture?'

Nobody warned her that menopause would ransack her hormones, leaving her a tired shell, wracked by sweeping fires on and on for years until they are so familiar that you greet them like old friends as you dig in your handbag for tissues to mop away the sweat.

The ancient sacred city of Anuradhapura nestles in intense green vegetation. Stone foundations and pillars mark the vestiges of a monastery that once housed five thousand monks in multi-storey hostels. In the distance, massive dagobas decorate the landscape like pure white breasts pointing towards the sky. This city thrived for over a thousand years, and the evidence is all around her, some excavated and marked, some lurking still forgotten in the long grass.

In the museum, she finds unearthed urinals: three large clay pots were stacked one on top of the other and buried in the ground. She presumes there must be holes in the bottom of the pots, but it is hard to see inside them, and the guide's English doesn't extend to the functionality of ancient urinals. On the other side of the veranda lies a hand-carved stone top for a pit latrine. Two carved feet mark where to squat over a key-shaped hole, and a sloping channel directs urine into the hole. Amazing, she thinks. Two thousand years ago these guys had better sanitation than half of the developing world today.

She wanders across the grass, trying to make sense in her head of the layout of the buildings, and nearly stumbles over a gigantic food trough. Carved from stone and the size of a large tree trunk, it fed five thousand monks at one sitting. Her mind strains to comprehend the logistics of such an establishment. Where did their food come from? Where were the crop fields, the orchards, the livestock pens? She can see where their water came from – numerous stone-walled, sunken reservoirs, some even partly filled by recent rain.

The city was supported by irrigated agriculture, she reads, with complex irrigation systems, some of which remain. She remembers the bubbling fountains of Sigiriya. What makes one culture develop extraordinary engineering skills and others not? What caused Sri Lanka to lose those skills and to sink from a rich and sophisticated culture with a written language, irrigation systems and excellent sanitation, to a war-torn Third World country with high levels of poverty?

Mind you, she thinks, the fact that the elite lived like this two thousand years ago, doesn't mean that there wasn't grinding poverty around them – the transient lives of the poor not marked by stone and brick, but dissolved back into the landscape on which they perched, precariously, for short and difficult lives.

A semi-circular carved stone decorates the entrance to the ruins of a small building. A lotus flower marks the centre of the half-circle, surrounded by concentric rings of images; a ring of water birds, possibly swans or geese, is followed by a ring of leaves. The next ring has elephants, lions, horses and bulls following each other. They symbolise the four stages of life, according to her brochure: growth, energy, power and forbearance. She wonders which animal represents which stage.

The final ring has a stylised design that the brochure describes as flames, though it looks more like the result of a psychedelic fantasy. She wonders what the use of psychedelic drugs was two thousand years ago in Sri Lanka as she looks around and tries to distinguish the skeleton of the vast ancient city between the verdant growth. Stone pillars, carved with mathematical precision, stand as sentinels where buildings once stood. They would have been plastered and painted then, supporting the multi-story wooden buildings. The wealth and effort that built this place must have been enormous.

Four walls, the brochure states, each twenty-six kilometres long, surrounded the city, which included the Sri Maha Bodhi tree, thought to be the oldest living tree in the world. That I must see, she thinks, looking around for signposts.

It is further than she thought, and when she finally finds herself outside the protective wall that surrounds the tree, she is damp with sweat. Above the walls, the leaves of what seems to be a ficus tremble in the breeze.

Wow, is this tree really two thousand years old? Impressive, she thinks and moves off to follow the signposts to the Ruwanwelisaya Dagoba with its stone elephants, magnificent white dome, and hidden relics. What is it in the human psyche, she wonders, that imbues ancient bits of bodies with such power? The Jetvanarama stupa, the largest stupa in the world, was built entirely to house a piece of a sash once worn by Buddha. One of Buddha's teeth is located somewhere around here. She wonders if it has more or less power than the pieces of the true cross, scattered in cathedrals across Europe, or the shady shroud of Turin. Which has resulted in the most miracles? It must be great to have that much faith, she thinks, to be able to believe that an old man with a long white beard has a plan for this violent, beautiful world. But if he does, why the hell did he allow so much violence, poverty and disease?

Somewhere nearby must be the Thuparamaya dagoba, surrounded by its two rows of stone pillars, which contains the collarbone of Buddha. Where is the rest of Buddha, and is the collarbone really still here if, as the guidebook says, the dagoba has been destroyed and rebuilt several times?

The Catholics perfected the art of relics, she muses, and turned it into good business. You could buy a piece of the true cross and never fall ill again. Or the tooth of St Bernard, the finger bone of St Thomas, the foreskin of the patron saint of HIV.

Bloody hell, it's hot and I'm tired. The prickles of a hot flush start in her neck and fingertips. Time for cool air and a drink, she thinks, and mops at the sweat trickling down the back of her neck.

Her meanderings have taken her past the fantastic white dagoba and on to the shore of a wide flat lake that once fed the paddies that provided the city with rice. A small brown bird fossicks amongst the reeds, and a white heron paces like an ageing judge through the shallows, watching minnows wriggle and flee.

# Musings on Beauty

An absurdly thin young woman called Sonja has painted Stella's face with sugar cane acid, and it is munching away at the dead skin cells that make her look older than she should. She lies on her back with her eyes closed, feeling her skin prickle and sting. She's getting used to it now. This is the fifth peel she's had, and she's up to fifty per cent strength. According to Sonja, her skin is getting used to it, so she can use a stronger acid. Stella's nose is tickling, and she grimaces, but the movement stabs itchy needles into the skin around her mouth, across her cheeks. She fights back the temptation to scratch.

Why on earth am I doing this? A pathetic attempt to stave off the wrinkles and stains of nearly sixty years of life, a victim of the expensive beauty myth that it is possible not to grow old. Well, not to look old, at least. The pain in her right hip reminds her that not even a face peel will turn the clock back. Perhaps she needs a hand peel too, the liver spots are a definite give away that she's been around the block more than once.

She sighs. What has she done over the past sixty years other than earning herself some liver spots and a bad hip?

She has done myriad things, had some fun, had some hard times, but has it all just been to fill space and time, or has she contributed something that might leave at least a little legacy behind? There is no child to remember her jokes and stories, no partner to mourn her when she dies.

The closest thing I had to a soul mate died more than half a lifetime ago. The world will barely notice it when I die. A slight gathering of the breeze as my breath joins it, and then, nothing.

Perhaps that's why people have children, she thinks, to defy mortality.

Nearly sixty years down, perhaps twenty left before the shadows of senility enter my mind, before my arthritic fingers struggle to replace the batteries in my hearing aids, and I must sit in pain, shut off from the world, questioning if it has all been worth it. It'll be paid old age care for me, she thinks, no children to pick me up when I fall over, visit me in hospital when I break my hip. Bloody wonderful future. If there is a god, she has a pretty sick sense of humour.

They ask job applicants to explain one of their greatest achievements. Yes, Stella, tell me about your greatest achievement? What have you achieved that you would like to tell us about? As she lies on her back with her face cracking and stinging, she is overwhelmed by the things she could have done, the missed opportunities. The children she chose not to have, the relationships she stifled that might have grown into something, the times she might have pushed herself to the front of the team, instead of taking a back seat. Maybe she could have taken up painting. Perhaps, if she'd been bolder, she could have set up her own company, acknowledged as someone to watch on the corporate ladder. She'd have liked the recognition.

Maybe having survived nearly sixty years of life largely intact is the greatest achievement of it all. It doesn't feel great.

Rather mundane. A bit like a sea sponge. Clinging on and hanging in no matter the tide. That's her achievement. A clinger and a hanger. But at least she hung on. She didn't give up.

A soft damp sponge gently attempts to wipe the age from her face.

# He's Back

He's back. The man who made her vomit her broken heart into the stained toilet bowl of her Hillbrow flat is back. In fact, he's ensconced on the sofa in her lounge, hands locked behind his head, long legs stuck out under the coffee table that her grandfather made so many moons ago. Even more moons ago than when she and Cedric were lovers, and that must have been…. twelve times thirty-five … at least four hundred and something moons ago.

God, that makes her feel old. Very, very old. As old as he looks, his paunch swelling over his too thin legs, his cropped hair a mixture of grey and silver above a thickened neck, double chin. She watches him, half waiting for a spark of the old desire to tickle the inside of her cranium, or better still, the soft flesh of her clitoris, just a little. Even the teeniest little bit. But there is nothing. Just a strange sense of time turning in an ever-widening spiral, and a faint sense of boredom.

'I've decided to climb Kili for my sixtieth,' he says. 'I'm still in pretty good shape, and I think it'll be great incentive to get into even better shape. Although I'm a bit worried about altitude sickness … I met this guy in Cape Town who was climbing a mountain in South America when he got hit by cerebral oedema. Had to come down as fast as possible. That worries me. You remember my dad died of a stroke at sixty, don't want to blow my own brain apart with altitude sickness. Hopefully, I'll be OK.'

She does remember his dad, although she doesn't remember him having died of a stroke. She's not sure if she ever knew that fact or whether she's just forgotten it. There's a lot she forgets these days. Quite often she can't remember if someone is alive or dead. His father was definitely alive all those moons ago. Not a particularly nice man, she thinks, arrogant, name-dropper, and a racist to boot. She was shocked to meet a racist coloured person. How naïve she was. Naïve enough to believe that Cedric the sexy would love her and stay true no matter what.

'Michele wants to come too. But I'm not sure about it. It's not like there's really a lot left between us these days. It's more like an arrangement, I guess. An arrangement in which I pay, and she takes.' There's a bitter edge to his voice, but nothing like the bitter taste in Stella's mouth.

Michele, the other woman. Well, the last of the other women, to be honest. The one he settled down with when she fell pregnant with the first of his four exquisite daughters. The one over whom her cracked heart fell into pieces and ended up with her spaghetti bolognaise in a stained toilet bowl. Penny. Tessa. Rochelle. And finally, Michele. Michele's patronising 1980's voice on the line from Durban: 'Hey, you need to be able to share, we can't do this love-as-property thing, you know. There is no ownership in love. We can be open in our relationships, you know, and let in so much more love.'

And semen. Into your womb, so that he was caught in parenthood and in love for you and there wasn't enough love to go around for me after all. What took her so fucking long to vomit him up and end it?

She leans back in her Gommagomma-clone armchair, relaxing. Several things occur to her. The first is that she doesn't have to talk. Doesn't even need to answer. He's quite capable of conducting a conversation all by himself. With himself. Poor Michele, she thinks. Thirty-five years of this? The second is that she doesn't care any longer, isn't even sure that she likes him. Certainly, he'd be more likable if he bothered to listen or ask about her for even just a moment. The third is that she doesn't really know why he is here, why he decided to phone her and drop round, but that it doesn't matter. She's travelling light for a change. She takes another mouthful of the Backsberg Merlot he brought along. At least the wine is good.

He's looking at her intently. Waiting for an answer. But she has no idea what he just said. Not the foggiest notion. 'Sorry,' she says and braves it out, 'I lost you for a moment there – lost in the mists of the past. What did you ask?'

'Andrew,' he says, 'what's happened to Andrew?'

'He lives in Jo'burg. Sandton, I think.'

'Illovo,' he corrects her. 'Beautiful place. I meant what happened to him? When did he become the corporate guy in a suit?'

'Oh god,' she laughs, 'years ago. The music didn't last. He always wanted the good things in life too much. What musician do you know who drives a Porsche?'

'He doesn't? Drive a Porsche, I mean? Really?'

'Really. Lots of horsepower beats a little blue pill any day. Pulls the babes too. Last time I saw him, he had a blonde half his age with him.'

Typical middle-aged man, she thinks, decorating his sleeve with young flesh, long legs, firm breasts. She slides her hand under her shirt and feels the roll of flab that hangs over the top of her trousers. None of the men her age are the least bit interested in her. She snorts. She's not even sexually interested in herself any longer. Why the hell would some man be? A Ben10. Maybe that's what she needs. Someone young and sexy and hot to decorate her own sleeve. Just like Cedric used to be, four hundred moons ago. Yeah. Right. Like anyone under fifty is going to be interested in her … But then again, what harm in trying. If she could work out where on earth to meet a sexy Ben10.

'So how is your work going – what exactly are you doing these days?'

Good god! He's asked her a question about herself, and he's looking at her as if he's interested in the answer. What took him so long?

'Still working as a consultant,' she responds. 'About twenty-five years now, I guess. Doing a fair amount of work outside South Africa. Quite a bit of travelling. Mainly in Africa but sometimes, I manage to get a bit of work further afield. India. I did some work in India. That was interesting. Ethiopia. I've been working on a project in Ethiopia. Love that. Such gentle people, and such awesome coffee. Wherever you go in Ethiopia, the coffee is awesome. It is the home of coffee after all! Not India. Indians make the shittiest coffee I've ever had. And I don't like tea. I've become a coffee snob – take my own coffee with me these days when I travel.'

'Wow, travelling to Gauteng is about as far as I get. Can't remember when last I left the country.'

'I love it. Not the airports. I can do without spending time in another airport. But getting to see other countries – that's the really lucky part. And someone else pays! I don't often get out of the main cities unless I organise a holiday, but even then, it's amazing. I did take a couple of days to explore Sri Lanka. That was special.'

'On your own?'

'Yeah. I've got used to it. I quite like it, actually. I can do what I want when I want without having to compromise.'

He watches her as if assessing how different this creature is from the one he knew so long ago. She realises how little they know each other, actors from a long-ago world come together again in a play that neither of them has read. She knows nothing of his loves and losses, his pains and triumphs, what he wants from life, what he aches for. A great sadness for what they have lost wells up in her.

'More wine?' she asks and bites back the rising past. 'I've got another bottle.'

# Being A Woman

Sometimes, thinks Stella, gazing at her bare feet, I don't feel very female. Not just not-feminine. More than that. Strangely genderless. Just me, neither male nor female. I wonder if that's a factor of menopause, she thinks. Or if it's just me. Maybe I should become one of those people who refuses to be called she. Or he. Maybe I should insist on being called they – although that doesn't work either, she muses, wiggling her red-painted toes. I don't feel plural. Maybe I should insist on being called it. That sounds appropriately gender neutral and singular. Or maybe I should just insist on being addressed in isiZulu, where there is no distinction between she and he. Fat lot of good that would do me, she thinks. I don't speak isiZulu!

She wiggles her toes again. Not even the fresh coat of fire-engine red makes her feel womanly tonight. She feels asexual, un-gendered, and a little lost. This wasn't on my menu when I grew up, she thinks. You were a boy or a girl. At least in her world. Do I really need, nearly six decades in, to wrestle with feeling genderless? Bloody menopause, even my identity feels shaken. She takes a long drink of ice-cold gin. Give me a couple of decades, she thinks, and I'll be truly genderless – bones in the ground. Or ash – that's truly genderless. Bones can still give you away.

Sometimes, Stella, she reminds herself, your mind does some very odd things. Best go to bed before you pour yourself another gin.

# Mogadishu

She places a slice of Peking duck onto the wafer-thin pancake, layers it with thinly sliced carrots, spring onions and a dash of orange and fennel sauce and takes a genteel bite. Delicious. She washes it down with a sip of Nederburg Merlot. The restaurant is busy and a background hum of conversation envelopes them.

Frank, recently back from Mogadishu, has the attention of the whole table, his grey eyes twinkling with laughter.

'So, there I am, in my wonderful bedroom ... in a container. We live in two rows of containers. With air conditioning, thank god. We'd die without it, curl up like little dried out frogs, overnight. Anyway, I'd just got there, and I didn't really know the routine. They'd given us a safety briefing, what to do if the siren sounds, how to keep your important goodies packed and ready to run, all of that. I'm lying in bed, just in my underpants, trying to sleep.'

Too much information, thinks Stella, imagining his slightly portly figure semi-naked in a steel container bedroom.

'Next thing I know, there's this massive thump. Sounds like it's next door. Takes me a while to work out where I am. Then I remember, I'm in a container in Mogadishu. There was a Ukrainian doctor next door – his rotation was over, and he was heading out that night. I assumed he was moving his furniture around or something, dropped his trunk on the floor. I don't know what I thought. I just rolled over and closed my eyes. Next thing the bloody siren goes off and there's another big thump. Oh shit. It's not the Ukrainian with his trunk, it's the Somalis with mortars.

'I've got this emergency bag packed – you have to have it ready – I grab my flak jacket and a bloody heavy helmet and I run for the bunker along with everyone else. I hammer in through the door, and I can tell you, my heart is pumping, my eyes must have been the size of soup plates. I get in through the door, and about twenty faces turn towards me and a whole bunch of them start to laugh. I'm standing there, clutching my bag, wearing my flak jacket, in my striped boxers and nothing else! It took a long time before they let me get over that one! The nurses still call me stripes!'

The table roars with laughter, wine glasses in hand.

'Why the hell are we laughing?' gasps Stella, 'you must have been terrified.'

'Yeah, well, you're pretty safe down there. There's a ton of concrete above you. It would take a fairly serious bomb to get through.'

'Jesus, it sounds like a war out there.' Rosalind sips her wine and gazes at Frank with wide-open eyes that look like the eyelids might flutter at any moment.

'It is a war up there,' comments Frank, gazing back.

Stella thinks of Jonny Steinberg's *A Man of Good Hope*, the story of a Somalian child who fled the violence in Mogadishu only to end up in the xenophobia of South Africa as an adult, his *spaza* shop burnt to the ground by the same people who were back to buy from him a week after the attack.

'I don't understand the desire to kill, to destroy, but perhaps that's what being middle class is about,' she says, 'being cushioned against the hunger and the violence that make people burn other poor people's shops. I've never known what it's like to be hungry, to not know where my next meal is coming from. I've never felt disregarded, ignored, irrelevant. Well, of course I have, I'm a woman, but not really, not like people on the edge of society.'

'That's only one side of the story, Stella,' Frank responds. 'The greatest violence comes from the middle class, those who allow their taxes to be used on guns, who make the guns, who plan the wars in which poor people lose their lives and their houses and their livelihoods.'

'Hey, Frank,' protests Rosalind, her eyelids no longer fluttering. 'You can't blame me for a civil war in Somalia!'

'Well,' Stella responds, surprising herself, 'according to Buddhist philosophy, we are all to blame. The Buddhists believe that everything is interconnected, and so somehow it is all dependent on us.'

'Since when are you a Buddhist?' Rosalind's non-fluttering eyelids are dangerously narrowed.

'I didn't say I was a Buddhist,' snaps Stella, just a little off kilter. 'But there is something there. I guess it's like the butterfly effect. You know, if a butterfly flaps its wings in Guatemala, it causes a storm in Delhi. I think it's an interesting idea.'

'I think you drank too much *rakshi* in Nepal! What is that stuff made of anyway?'

'Millet. Home distilled. Kicks like a yeti.'

'I'll stick to wine, thanks. Shall I order another bottle?'

That night, the image of Frank in his striped boxers, stretched out on a bed in a container room in Mogadishu, won't leave her.

She imagines herself lying next to him, their ageing bodies protected from the heat and the war outside. She feels his hands caress her, enjoying the weight of her breasts, feels him fondle her no longer slender waist, stroke her thighs, his hands celebrating her multiple curves. She pictures their two worn and flabby bodies as they touch in the cool air, the frisson of desire. She slides her fingers between her legs and imagines they are Frank's, feels his tongue against her nipples as his body presses against hers.

It has been a long time since she felt such desire. Her nipples tighten, she spits on her fingers to moisten her clit, and relaxes deep down into the pleasure of her own body.

# Christmas

It's that day again. December 25th. The day on which families gather, join happy congregations to praise the Lord, exchange presents, eat too much, drink too much, and sit around with bloated stomachs reminiscing and moaning about the state of the world.

For Stella, it is none of these. It is a day of aloneness, of sometimes aching loneliness. Her family doesn't gather for Christmas. Sandra spends it with the in-laws in their glass and chrome beach house in Plett, and Stella does not intend to spend it alone with her mother listening to repeated stories of Stella's allegedly golden childhood.

How plastic our memories are, Stella muses, made and remade in our own image over time. We believe with such conviction in what we remember, and our memories are like stories, passed down through millennia, changed in each telling. Each time we recall a memory it changes, and we save it, edited, revised. We even change the feelings associated with the memories. So the experts say.

Can we then, ponders Stella, take a sad memory and, through a positive retelling, turn it into a happy memory? Can I reconstruct for myself the happy memories of my childhood that my mother has? If I take a memory – Mum telling insecure teenage me, just about to brave a party, that I was too fat and that my dress made me look like a sack of potatoes – can I turn that into a happy memory?

Just how plastic are our memories?

If I work on it long enough, can I change it to remember instead, my mother telling me how beautiful I was in my caftan, how much the hippy look suited me, how proud she was of me? If memories are plastic, can we consciously and deliberately change them? Can I create a pain-free past?

How would that work, she wonders? I enter the lounge where my parents sit, smoking and reading. Yes, they both smoked. This was the seventies after all. Which is why I was wearing a kaftan! My mother lifts her head up from her book and smiles at me.

'You look gorgeous, Stella. What pretty fabric. And your hair really suits you like that. Are you off to see Fred?'

'Roger Lucey. *The Road is Much Longer* concert.'

'Oh, that, yes. Have fun.' Even reconstructing the memory it is hard to avoid her mother's tone of mild disapproval. She rewinds, rethinks.

'Going to listen to Roger Lucey. *The Road is Much Longer* concert.'

'That sounds fun. Have a wonderful evening.' And she hits save before her mother can add, 'Don't do anything silly, dear.'

And now, she thinks, when I remember that evening in future, what will I remember? The reconstructed memory? Or myself reconstructing the memory? Or some partly changed version of the original memory?

And how will I know that the memory has changed in any way unless I write it down now and check back when I remember it next time. And if I check back in my diary and find the original version of the story, written down, then which will I remember, the written version or the edited version? And at what stage will my brain just start to give an error reading?

Odd, she thinks. It is much easier just to believe that what we remember is what happened. Life is complex enough without the realisation that you don't remember with any accuracy what has happened to you over the past nearly sixty years.

Despite reconstructed and unreconstructed memories, Christmas remains a desolate affair for Stella, and this year the loneliness feels rooted in her pelvis, the fulcrum of her body, so that she can barely stand upright. Coiled in her faux Gommagomma chair she watches *Grey's Anatomy* Season Three and sobs until the sobs turn into wails and she has become a primal beast alone in a bleak wilderness, howling for a mate, for someone to hold her and love her and tell her she is wonderful and funny and intelligent and special.

As ambulances come and go the howls subside and she is left puffy eyed and alone, watching love affairs rise and collapse in a ten-year-old medical soapie. Tears trickle down her face and drip from her chin. Is this what life is? Watching soapies alone on Christmas day? She puts aside the computer and heads for the kitchen for another gin and tonic.

At least alcohol hasn't left me, she thinks, Lady Drink remains a constant companion, in sickness and in health, for richer, for poorer, till death us do part. The ice clinks against the glass, the tonic hisses as she opens it. Some things don't change, she thinks. Like gin and tonic. And loneliness.

# The Man at the Gate

There's a young man at the gate. His worn jeans barely cling to his skinny hips, lank hair frames an already raddled face and pathetic eyes.

'I just want to go home, ma'am,' he says, 'I just want to go home.'

'I'll give you food, but I'm not giving you money,' Stella responds.

'Ma'am, thank you ma'am, but I want to go home to my mother. I want to go back home. Please, ma'am.'

'I'll give you food, but I'm not giving you money,' Stella repeats, annoyed. There are tears in his eyes. Oh god, not the emotional blackmail trick, she thinks. I've seen that one too often.

'Please, ma'am, I won't ask you again, but I really want to go home. I want to get better. At home.'

Yeah right, she thinks, you want money for your next fix. She hands over a tin of fish, half a loaf of low GI bread, and thirty Rand.

'Thank you, ma'am, thank you so much.' The tears threaten to spill down his grimy cheeks. 'Could you perhaps just give me another fifteen Rand? Then I can get a taxi home. To Bronkhorstspruit, ma'am.'

'Don't push your luck,' snaps Stella and walks back into the house leaving the tearful youngster at her gate with his

fish and bread and enough money to get him not quite home,
or a cheap bottle of wine.

# Office Politics

Stella is outraged. Her space feels violated. Which is odd, because it hasn't affected her at all really. Someone has stolen the petty cash. One of the eleven of them in the office. She casts her mind around the staff to look for opportunity and motive. Yeah, well, motive is easy; everyone is tempted by cash, and she knows only too well that it isn't always the poor who succumb to temptation. The cash went missing between Friday lunchtime and Monday morning before ten.

She cuts to the chase like a latter-day Rizzoli: that means that Tony, Mzala, Sarah and Tumi are excluded. And herself of course. She can rule herself out, although she does hope that everyone else realises she should be ruled out. It makes her feel a little uneasy that she might be on the general list of suspects.

And she guesses you could exclude Fezile, who is in the office manager's office, shocked and scared. You'd have to be fairly brazen to steal 2000 Rand and then tell people it had been stolen. Or would you? It would be a clever way to cover your tracks – steal the money and put the blame elsewhere. Although Fezile said that someone had been nicking small amounts for over a year. She'd paid out of her own pocket to cover it up so that no one would blame her for being lousy at managing the petty cash. Although that could be just a good story too.

Stella sighs. She recalls her recent flight back from India. Three and a half hours to Dubai, two hours in the busy glitz of Dubai airport and eight glorious, isolated hours on the plane back to ORT. No anxiety, no politics, nothing to worry about except whether she would finish *A Walk in the Woods* before the plane landed. She wanted to find out if Bill Bryson made it to the end of the Appalachian Trail. It seemed unlikely considering how much of the trail was left and how far into the movie she was. As it turned out, he didn't. But he did survive it.

Now she asks herself whether she'd picked up the cash that she'd left on her desk before the trip, or whether someone else had. She's never worried about these things before, had left her handbag on her desk when she was in the boardroom or the loo. It was, after all, only the eleven of them. But now one of them is a thief.

She reaches for a lemon cream from the small bowl of biscuits she filled up in the tea room and pushes away the memory of her early morning promise while staring at the array of too-small clothes in her cupboard, not to eat junk today.

Three people come in early, she thinks. It could have been one of them. Alice works in the office where the petty cash is kept. Opportunity definitely present. Motive? Low salary would do it, and two kids and an ailing aunt to support. Phola? A taste for expensive clothes and fancy hairstyles. Earns a decent salary but spends a lot. Zara just bought a ridiculously expensive car. Rich daddy helps with the car, of course, but being rich isn't a sinecure for honesty. Rich people just steal in larger amounts, thinks Stella, and they can afford the lawyers to get away with it.

The cash from her desk nags at her. She can't remember having picked it up from her desk and put it in her bag. She tries to remember how much it was – around 140 Rand? The change from the courier for a photocopy of their grandmother's recipe for her cousin, Mandy, in Cape Town. Rich, selfish Mandy. Stella still hasn't forgiven her for selling the only portrait of their maternal grandmother. Just because it didn't fit with the look prescribed by her interior decorator, or her Ben10, as her ex-husband called him. Why did I courier the book? I should have sent it COD.

She turns back to her screen, resolutely ignores the flashing new email icon and squares up to the blank space under 'Executive Summary'. She hates executive summaries. What is the point of a sixty-page report if you can sum it up in ten? Just to provide everyone with an excuse not to read the full sixty pages. Might as well just write a ten-page report and get it over with. She scrabbles in her bag for her earphones. Mozart. The only option she has to get through the Executive Summary on time. Piano Concertos. Loud.

And more coffee.

# Going East

Stepping off the plane is like cracking open the skin of a pomegranate, feeling the sting of anticipation of the tight red jewels inside, the spurt of juice in her mouth. China, ancient, modern, mystical, political, other. The expectation burns on her tongue.

A black and yellow Hyundai whisks her into an ocean of cars and bicycles moving with chaotic order. After the abrasive klaxons of South African taxis, the hoots seem muted, polite. A man transporting a bundle of reinforcing rods twice the length of his bicycle weaves steadily through the traffic, avoids a pristine black Mercedes that turns in front of him. A huddle of young women in *takkies* and neat skirts, faces hidden by paper masks against the pollution, wait to cross at the busy intersection. High-rise buildings stretch up to a grey sky.

They crawl past incomprehensible street signs and busy office blocks, avoiding pedestrians, bicycles and swathes of cars until they reach her hotel. She chokes back a splutter of laughter. A pachydermous and incongruous faux-rock façade has been plastered over half of the hotel. It looks precarious as if the fibre-glass rocks might come loose at any minute and tumble ten storeys onto the busy road below. She is grateful that the entrance is through the half of the hotel that, bizarrely, has been allowed to remain painted concrete and glass.

The cancerous-looking artificial rock, to her relief, has failed to ooze through the windows, and once inside, apart from the neat young women in silk dresses, their black hair tied up in chignons or falling in perfect alignment alongside their pale cheeks, she could be in a Holiday Inn in any part of the world. There is a comforting, if boring, familiarity in her surroundings. She glances at her watch, tries to orient her body in the new time zone. She has three hours before the welcome dinner.

Over jet lag, quails' eggs and shark fin soup, she learns the meaning of *gambai* and matches her hosts drink for drink with a mild amusement at her ability to toss back a tot at a time. All that training on gin, she thinks, feeling more than a little woolly around the edges. It is the only next morning that she learns the real consequences of too much gambai with sixty-five per cent proof *baijiu*. She never knew rice spirits could kick so hard.

She knocks back two Myprodol, pulls on a smart black jacket and black court shoes, avoids breakfast in honour of her unhappy liver and heads out to look for a taxi.

The Beijing Water Authority has pulled out all stops, and she finds herself seated at a dark wood boardroom table with six Chinese engineers, three of whom, including the chairperson, she's delighted to see, are female. She feels a little under-equipped though, not being an engineer.

The presentations are highly technical, and she is confused by the numbers. It takes a while for her to understand that the Chinese count in hundreds of thousands, or tens of millions, not in thousands and millions. Once she's got that dissonance sorted, she is fascinated by the presentations, overwhelmed by the depth of skills and the vast capacity for implementation of the Chinese. She makes notes and listens. Listens and makes notes. And drinks endless cups of herbal tea.

Engineer Hu talks about the planning and construction of the Three Gorges Dam. It involved the relocation of over 1.3 million people and twenty-six million cubic metres of concrete, but Stella can't tear her eyes from Engineer Hu's face, the exquisite Modigliani line from cheekbone to chin as she turns her head, the peach-soft perfection of her skin. Twenty-six turbine generator sets, says the perfect mouth, generation capacity of 18.2 million kilowatts. Black hair swings softly against the pale skin of her neck.

Concentrate, thinks Stella and tries hard to focus on taking notes and doodling spirals and whorls instead. Jetlag. This must be jet lag.

At dinner that night, they are served mandarin fish, baked whole in a light pastry scored into diamonds that glisten in the elegant restaurant lighting. She half wonders if it is an endangered species, but a second glass of rice wine sets her mind at ease, and she finds herself trying to explain South African politics through the haze of alcohol and linguistic confusion that drapes the table.

'Our president is corrupt,' she says. 'He's in bed with a dreadful family from India.'

'In bed?' Chang asks.

'It's a phrase we use,' she laughs. 'It means he's got very close ties with them. He makes decisions to serve their interests. And his own. He doesn't care about the people, just that he and his friends get rich. Oh, and he wants to avoid going to jail with all of the corruption charges facing him, so he wants to bring his ex-wife in as the next president so she can protect him.'

Chang laughs. 'How much money has he stolen? In China, he would face a firing squad.'

'Not a bad idea,' she responds. 'Except that our Constitutional Court ruled the death penalty to be unconstitutional.'

'No death penalty?' Hu asks, incredulous.

'No death penalty.' There is a moment of silence around the table before Chang splashes more Laobai Fenjiu into their glasses.

'Gambai,' and a sting in her throat from the slap of the white spirit and scent of fruity paraffin hanging in the air, the moment is past. As the burn hits her stomach she grieves for what has become of her country.

# Meaning of Life

A gaggle of Orthodox Jews is on the flight, in baggy black coats like leftovers from an Oxfam shop. Across the aisle, a young man wears a black plastic strip twisted round his left arm and hand, ending in a series of twists around his middle finger. More black plastic strips hold a small black box on his forehead. Stella knows they have deep religious meaning, but in the artificial light of a 737, they strike her as a peculiar form of bondage. Or fetishism. Where does fetishism stop, and religious fervour start?

Perhaps the presence of a god determines the difference. And fetishism generally has sexual implications and from the looks of this guy, his brand of fetishism is not sexual. He's kept his eyes down since they stepped into the slowly moving security check line as if afraid to glance at a world of voluptuous African women. But then, who knows, Stella chuckles to herself – perhaps he's a tempest in bed after his prayers are done and the candles are blown out.

And then the other tribe arrive, a Muslim family, three women wrapped in black shrouds, only their dark eyes and the gold jewellery on their elegant fingers indicating the living bodies underneath.

She wonders what the Torah and the Koran teach about the sexual needs and desires of women and whether bringing your partner to orgasm is an act of celebration of the glory of god, or not. After all, if god made women, she must have put the clitoris there for a purpose.

What does that make female genital mutilation of the kind they practice in parts of the Horn of Africa? Where they cut away the clitoris? An act of the devil? An anti-god act?

Her thoughts ramble as the ancient religious traditions of this part of the world, embodied in the white scarves of women in the Orthodox Ethiopian church, the black hats and coats of Orthodox Jews, the swathed bodies of Muslim women, press in on her psyche and evoke a deep questioning, not of the meaning of life. She has long accepted that there is little meaning to life. Life just is, and you choose to get on with it, or you don't.

She ruminates on what human fragility needs faith in a god or gods. Perhaps with an invisible friend, you are never lonely, never confronted with the fundamental existential principle that you are always, always alone. I could do with that, thinks Stella. Tough being a sceptic. Tough not having an invisible friend.

She looks down through the night sky, and, as if conjured out of a dream, a pale-yellow half-moon hangs in the blackness below her. I am above the moon, she mumbles, surprised, and absurdly delighted by the thought.

# The Colour of her Skin

Stella has a flashback, to a workshop in KwaZulu Natal where she sat with a group of small tree farmers (tree farmers with small farms, not people farming small trees, or small people farming trees) discussing their challenges in getting licences from the government to grow trees. They complained of multiyear delays that crippled them economically or forced them to grow trees illegally. It had been a long and hot day. The portable air-conditioner in the pre-fab office could not cope with the press of bodies and the blistering summer sun – and she was exhausted but stimulated by the challenge of trying to solve real problems for real people.

Suddenly, as if looking down from above, she saw that she was the only white person in the room. With a strange sense of joy, she realised that she has been working all day without consciousness of race, just one of a group of people trying to solve a common problem.

For a white South African, born into apartheid, racial discrimination taken in with her mother's milk, it was a moment of intense liberation. She was just a person, working with other people who needed her assistance. In that moment, she was not defined by the colour of her skin.

In front of a workshop full of anticipation in Dire Dawa, she realises that once again she is the only white person in the room. Indeed, for the whole week in Ethiopia, she hasn't engaged with a single other white person. She feels her shoulders lighten a little, and the burden of colonial history lifts for a moment and allows her to be just an African, trying to solve African problems together with her African brothers, and a few, very few, sisters.

She looks at the predominantly male group in front of her and feels her shoulders sink again. How long will it take before women and men are equal on this continent? She remembers that this part of the world is one of the hotspots of female genital mutilation, and she shudders. Menopausal, her libido fading, she is still very grateful to her clitoris, which intermittently brings her moments of shuddering, soul churning pleasure. She can't imagine the horror of having it cut out, as a child, the pleasure of orgasm replaced by years of pain and infection.

'… report on improved cook stoves …'

She snaps her mind back to energy issues in Ethiopia and flushes as she finds herself in front of a group of expectant eyes. She wonders if there is a question she needs to answer, not quite sure what the next step is. The speaker continues, in his soft, accented voice, '... but we haven't done anything on improving the charcoal production process, and there is a lot to be done in that regard.'

Her heart slows to normal. She's back in the room, back on track, issues of race packed into a safe corner of her mind.

'I'm interested in the statistics,' she probes. 'Can you tell me why in some areas they use wood and in other areas they prefer charcoal?'

'In the areas where the staple food is pasta, they like using wood,' ventures a young woman at the end of the table, so quietly that Stella must walk towards her and cup her hand behind her ear to hear better. 'Where they cook injera, they prefer using charcoal.'

'Amazing,' she responds. 'So current energy use choices are the result of colonial food practices?' Twenty pairs of eyes stare at her as if at a small green creature from a red planet. She smiles again and shifts gear. 'I'm told people would rather cook injera on traditional stoves than on electric stoves? Is that right?'

'They taste better,' responds a middle-aged man with quiet dignity at the other end of the room. 'Even when people can afford electric stoves, injera tastes better cooked the traditional way.'

# New Year's Eve

She's in Club VSP in Sandton, against her better judgement. Mark has persuaded her to come with him but he's vanished into the gloom and flashing lights in search of something to snort. Perched on a high bar stool she nurses a double gin and tonic and watches people having fun and preparing for midnight. There must be thirty couples on the dance floor, in various stages of intoxication by various means.

She's sure the tall thin couple on the left are on something, maybe ecstasy. How would she know? They've been dancing, entwining and disentangling, since she sat down. Their rhythm shifts, adjusting to the changing tracks and the flashing lights that sweep over them and trace their tangled bones in streaks of green and red.

Behind them are two men. One gyrates and bops to the bone trembling beat, the other follows, like an early android, stiff, embarrassed, a fraction behind the beat. She wonders what kind of rhythm they find together in bed.

She looks around for Mark. Typical, she thinks. Bring me somewhere I don't want to be and then dump me. Bastard. And we came in his car, so I'm trapped. Her thumb hovers over the Uber app when she notices a woman watching her from the other end of the bar. It's like looking down a tunnel into a raging fire.

She turns back to the dance floor. The two men have left, and a young woman in a bum-hugging red dress twirls around and around, arms held high to the sounds of Faithless.

A soft bump startles Stella as the eyes from the other end of the bar slide up onto the cherry red plastic and chrome seat next to her.

'Hi, can I buy you a drink?' Stella freezes like a kudu in the headlights.

'Umm, I have one, thanks.' She gulps at her gin.

'Terri.'

'Sorry?'

'I'm Terri.'

Terri's eyes are light green, ringed by a dark border. They stroke over Stella's face and rest on the pulse that has started to pound in the hollow at the base of her throat.

'Stella,' she mutters and clears her throat.

Terri sips on a cloudy cocktail, torn mint leaves floating amongst the crushed ice. A soft black t-shirt covers strong shoulders, soft, rounded breasts. An oval of turquoise framed in silver hangs from her neck, matched by small blue drops in her ears. Her smile crinkles the crow's feet around her eyes, lifts the lines of experience around her sensual mouth.

What do you see in me? Stella wants to ask.

'If you don't mind me saying so,' Terri ventures, her smile just a little tentative, 'you are very sexy.' She sips her *mojito* and watches Stella over the rim of her glass.

Stella is mesmerised. She stands on a cliff high above a still, green pool. She feels the tug of gravity pulling her towards the edge. She trembles on the brink. The water is bottomless and dark. A wave of panic pulls her back.

'Excuse me,' she says, 'I have to find someone.' And she steps away and into the flashing lights and swaying bodies.

# Mother

Stella's mother is coming to visit. The idea doesn't make her happy. Generally, she keeps as far from her mother as possible. It's complex. More complex than Stella likes to admit, and the fact that her 85-year-old mother has arranged herself a lift to Johannesburg and has invited herself to stay with Stella has resulted in an even stiffer gin than usual.

At least, since the troglodyte moved out, the spare room is once again white and tidy, and the smell of smoke has gone from the pillows and duvet after The Angel washed them in hot water and left them hanging in the sun for a day. The Angel also scrubbed the floor, threw out a rubbish bag of beer cans and a torn pair of underpants that had been used to wipe up spilt beer.

Stella breathes a huge, deep sigh of relief at the silence that envelops the house and ponders on how her strict sister had managed to bring up such a careless creature. Lazy, actually. Dirty and lazy. What the hell had Sandra done as a mother? Stella knows that she'd make a dreadful mother, too impatient, selfish and demanding. Limited maternal instinct, really, but to her surprise, after a day or two, she'd started to miss the roar of Airbourne from the spare room, the sound of feet down the passage at strange times of the night, the ravenous devouring of whatever food she stocked in the kitchen.

In the silence, she tastes a faint sense of loss and a smidgeon of envy for Sandra. She turns on her iPad and Tracy Chapman pushes away the silence.

Please put towels in spare room, she writes on the whiteboard in the kitchen, new soap, toilet paper – my mother is coming to stay.

Oh god, she thinks, my mother. For a week. My mother who taught me that guests, like fish, go off after three days. Just because she's family, does she think it doesn't apply? What am I going to do with her for a week? I'd better stock up on whisky, that's for sure. She'll get through a serious amount of whisky in a week. Johnny Walker is sufficient. If she wants Tullamore, she can buy it herself.

Oh bloody hell, she thinks, I don't have a TV. I never replaced it when the tube blew. Moved into the realm of Showmax and news streaming, instead of a flat screen with DSTV. What is the old bat going to do all day without Discovery Channel and *Law and Order/CSI/Blue Bloods/Criminal Minds*?

She must have been a detective in a previous life. Or maybe a criminal – a devious, manipulative criminal mastermind. Easy Stella, she remonstrates with herself. It's just your mother coming to stay, not Charles Manson!

Two days later, as the storm clouds drag an ominous purple light out of the west, a blue Qashqai pulls up outside the house. A neatly groomed man in jeans and his mid-thirties smiles at Stella in what she imagines to be a mildly exhausted fashion, while her mother waits for someone to open the door for her.

Here we go, thinks Stella.

'Thank you so much for bringing her up, it's so kind of you. Would you like to come in for something to drink?' Please come in and dilute the mother-effect.

'Thanks, but I really do need to get home. Your mother has been very sweet. She's a wonderful woman.''

'Yes, isn't she.' Capable of creating great wonder. Wondering how to get through a week of her company. Wondering how she manages to be so snide in so few words. Wondering where she got her amazing sense of entitlement. Wondering why no one else sees through her perfectly styled hair and elegant manner to the ruthless, demanding shrew below.

'Hi, Mum. Lovely to see you. Let's get you out and into the house.' My god, thinks Stella, she's so old and fragile. Is it really that long since I last saw her?

'Hello, Stella, my dear, you look tired. Peter, would you mind carrying my suitcase and my walker inside? Stella, you'll have to help me up the steps, dear. My legs aren't what they used to be.'

Peter, obedient and smiling, carries the walker, a suitcase, a large handbag and a blue cooler bag up the steps and into the house.

'Last room on the right,' Stella calls out, holding her mother's arm as she shuffles and with great effort, up the three steps from the street, into the yard and along the path to the front door. The arm under her fingers is dry and light, the skin slightly cold like a desiccated aloe leaf. Stella feels her fingers, like snails' horns, wanting to retreat from the touch, but she tightens her grip as her mother steps inside her house.

'It's fine, dear, I'll use my walker now.' But Stella is loath to let go, to let this frail but cataclysmic force loose in her house. Filled with misgivings, she lets her hand fall to her side and watches her mother shuffle into the lounge and straight towards Stella's armchair.

A great start, thinks Stella. Must be a record. Not even three minutes and she's taken over my space. 'Can I get you some tea, Mum?'

'What's the time?' The old woman squints at her wristwatch.

'Quarter past six.'

'Then I'll have a whisky, There's a bottle in my briefcase.'

No wonder it weighs so much. An unopened bottle of Tullamore Dew nestles amongst papers, packets of tissues and bottles of pills. It feels invasive to look in her mother's briefcase like this. She grabs the whisky from the case and two heavy bottomed, delicately rounded tumblers from the cabinet.

One block of ice. No water. And a more generous dose for herself.

'How was the trip?'

'What a sweet young man. He's Jenny's nephew. He comes down to visit her once a month. His mother was Jenny's sister. She died of cancer two years ago. So now he visits Jenny instead. Says she's like his second mother. Such a sweet man. So caring and responsible.'

Guilt stabs Stella just where she imagines her mother wanted it to. Not even her son but he visits … ''It looked like a comfortable car?'

'Very comfortable. Cheers.'

The whisky is good. It slides down her throat and settles comfortingly into her stomach, spreads into her veins and her brain. Stella takes another large sip and sighs. It's going to be a long week, but at least the whisky is good.

'Did I tell you about Patrick?''

Of course you didn't, Stella snaps in silence, we've hardly spoken to each other for years. Who the hell is Patrick? Another of Jenny's too-good-to-be-true nephews?

'The young man who mows my lawn. Well, all of our lawns, really. He's from Zimbabwe. He's got a BSc. Can you believe that? He's got a BSc and he can't get a job. He's illegal, of course. They all are. But so sad that he can't get a decent job. Really, it's terrible what that man has done to that country.'

Don't start, Mum, Stella begs inwardly. Please don't start on the African dictator rant. I haven't had nearly enough whisky yet. But Marge is off on a different track this time.

'So, Sally's grandson, she's the one who lives just behind me, the one whose husband left her for the neighbour. You remember? Her grandson struggles with science at school. Shame, I don't think he's very bright. So, I suggested to her that maybe Patrick could help out, and so he started giving Logan extra lessons. And Logan did so well that other kids wanted Patrick's help as well. And now the school has taken him on to give extra lessons. All quite illegal of course, but really, it's such a waste of talent not to use him. I'm so happy for him.'

Mum the hero, thinks Stella. Always fixing things for everyone. And making sure everyone knows. Dammit. She does do good stuff. Why can't I be more generous?

'That's amazing, well done!' But her smile is plastic and her words hollow, and she hopes that a bit more whisky will help to mask her from herself.

'Supper?' she asks. 'I have hand-made pasta and pesto. Not my hands. But pretty good.'

'That sounds lovely, dear. A little fattening, but can't do any harm once in a while.'

*Aaaargh,* screeches Stella in the echoing chambers of her mind. Leave my bloody weight out of this. For once! And she crashes the pot onto the stove.

'Is everything OK?' calls her mother from the lounge.

'Fine, just fine. No problem at all.'


It's been two days and Stella has managed to keep herself, sufficiently busy that she only has to engage with her mother over drinks and supper. She doesn't know what her mother does during the day, and she doesn't really care, although she has a faint suspicion that it involves scrabbling through her drawers. She wouldn't put it past the woman who read her teenage diary and hauled her secret desires out in conversation with a bunch of her friends who'd dropped round for tea.

Perhaps they were the most exciting things in her life, thinks Stella bitterly, my dreams of becoming a famous actress. My crush on Clint Eastwood. She laughs at her teenage self, but the sense of betrayal remains. She can hear the laughter of the housewives of Durban North, feels again how her fragile self cracked, just where her heart was meant to be.

They're sitting in the lounge with the usual glass of whisky each, the level in the bottle already low after only two days. Stella doesn't remember her mother downing quite so much whisky in the evenings.

She drivels on about a work project until her mother cuts through her words like a broomstick in the spokes of a bicycle.

'Stella, I have something to tell you.'

Stella pulls herself back into equilibrium. Here we go again, she thinks. She never did bloody listen to a word I said.

'I'm sorry to interrupt you, but I need to get this off my chest.'

What, she apologised for interrupting? Well, that's a first.

'I'm not sure how to tell you this, so I'll just be blunt.' Which was ever your way, Mother.

'I have cancer. Liver cancer. It's metastasized. Not much hope I'm afraid.'

For a nano-second, the foundations of the house turn to jelly, and Stella grabs at the arms of her chair.

'They say I've got between three months and a year left. Not that they really know, of course. There's nothing they can do. It's too far gone, and I'm too old for some of the more radical treatment options. Not worth wasting their time trying to save this old body.' Her mother smiles through the sadness.

Stella's mouth is a desert, the crack around her heart aching in a manner she is not used to.

'So, my dear, I've made a plan. There's a group in Switzerland called … called … damn it, what is it called. That place where they help you to die.'

'Assisted suicide? You're planning an assisted suicide? There must be some alternative. This is crazy.' Words flood into the desert and jam in her mouth in their haste.

'Actually, they call it accompanied suicide. It's a much nicer name, don't you think. So you're not alone in your last moments.'

We are always alone, especially when we die. 'Mum, I don't know what to say.'

'You never were very good with that.'

'With what?'

'Finding the right words to say.'

Thanks, Mum, we're talking about your death and you still manage to get a dig in. Never fucking fails, does it? Not even liver cancer can stop you.

'But never mind that. I have a request. I want you to come with me. I want you and Sandra to be there when I die. I've already contacted them. I want to go next month. I've already spoken to Sandra. I'll pay for the whole trip, don't worry about that.'

'Sandra knows? She's agreed to this? This is a stupid plan.'

'No, Stella.'

God, I hate your condescension, dammit,

'This is not a stupid plan. This is my choice, and as it will be my last act, I'm asking you, for once, to put someone else first and do what I ask. My dying wish, if you want to be sentimental.'

Stella's mind reels, battered. She reaches for the bottle and pours them each a stiff couple of fingers. Tears fight against her willpower and threaten to wash her away, tears for the loss of her mother, tears for the ancient loss of the mother she wished she'd had, the tender, gentle, warm mother her friends seemed to have. She's angry too, but in too much turmoil to do much other than try to hold her emotions at bay.

'I'm asking for a week of your time. To fly over – we can go business class.' Her mother chuckles. 'It's not as though I'll have much use for the money later! There are two counselling sessions and then they'll give me a poisoned chalice, and that will be it. I'd really like you to be there.'

To Stella's consternation, the tears win and pour down her cheeks while she gasps for breath like a goldfish out of water.

'It's all right, dear,' her mother says, 'no need to cry. I've made my peace with this. I've had a long life. It is better this way than lying in a hospital with tubes and monitors while they eke out my last hours in a haze of morphine. It's not a pleasant way to go, you know, liver cancer.'

Stella looks through a blur of tears at the frail old woman in the big armchair. Christ, she thinks, she picked me apart, undermined me, made me feel not quite good enough my whole fucking life, and now she sits there, like a shrunken crow, and asks me to do the hardest thing imaginable and I'm torn apart by how much I love her despite the anger. She takes a big slug of whisky.

'You don't have to say anything now. Just think about it.'


Even after an extra stiff nightcap, Stella can't sleep. She can hear the weak snores of her mother as if the walls have turned to tissue paper. For all her travels, this was not a journey she had thought of making, yet. She'd hoped that by the time her time came, the law would have changed, and she could choose the time and place of her own death, in her own country. She's bewildered that her mother has made this choice before her. She always thought the old woman would cling on till the bitter, sans everything, end.

Panic claws at her throat as she thinks of a trip with her mother and her sister. She breathes through the claustrophobia and back into the night. This is an emotional landscape she has eschewed for decades, unfamiliar now, and pockmarked with landmines that might blow her carefully constructed life to hell. In a handbasket, she thinks, angry now.

That's what mothers do, she thinks. They mess with your life as a kid and then they think they can come back and mess with it again. And again. And that you'll love them through it all. Because that's what we do. We love our mothers.

Mother's love gives a woman the power to lift a car off her child, to smash down a door to get to her child locked inside, to take the bullet first. A child's love for her mother is much more complicated, she thinks, at least in my case. I'm not at all sure that I'd take a bullet for her. Would I do that for a child, if I'd had one? Is that why I didn't have children? Too selfish? Or was it that I didn't want to be like her, didn't want to repeat her on my own children. Someone has to break the cycle. The tears prick at her eyes again. Who are you crying for? Yourself? Her? Or the children you never had?

The snores nag at her now, catch at the edge of her consciousness and drum against her brain. She turns on a YouTube meditation video and the nasal twang of some Australian silences the snores and calms her busy head.

You have to do it, she thinks, just before she drifts off to sleep. You have to do it. There isn't an option.

# The Heart Breaks

She is brushing her teeth when the pain strikes like a bicycle spoke into her heart – no blood, no mess, just a pain that makes her drop the toothbrush, press her hand against her heart and stare, wide-eyed, into the mirror.

Oh, Jesus, she thinks, as adrenaline surges through her body. Is this what a heart attack feels like?

Mortality stares back from the mirror, pale, baggy-eyed, skin patchworked with sunspots and the passage of time. She rinses her mouth, one hand still pressed against the pain, and staggers through to perch, uncertain, on the edge of her bed.

I don't want to die.

Thank god my mother has gone. I don't need her to see this. It'll be Sinah who finds me. She'll come in to sweep and she'll find me lying here, dead. A bit more than she can sweep up.

Hospital, she thinks. I'd better get myself to hospital. I don't want to die.

In casualty, they insist on admitting her – heart pain is not taken lightly by the medical profession, and she lies between crisp white sheets and listens to the beep and bustle of the hospital. By the time the doctor gets to her, the pain has passed and she is bored.

'I'm fine,' she says to the young Xhosa woman. 'Really, I'm fine now.'

'I'm sorry,' the woman responds as she tucks her stethoscope back into her pocket, 'we need to keep you in overnight.'

'Is something wrong?'

'No, it all seems fine now, it was probably just stress, it can do that. But it's hospital policy with heart problems. We'll just keep you in for observation. Just for the night.' And she is gone, leaving Stella alone between the crisp white sheets.

Sartre was wrong, thinks Stella, hell isn't other people. Hell is spending an unnecessary night amidst the sterile bleeps and bells of a hospital, without even the comfort of a book. I suppose I should be comforted by the fact that I am not going to die. Not just yet.

Unlike my mother.

# The Litho Print

She's drunk again. The kind of two-glasses-of-wine edges-rubbed-off-the-world kind of drunk. Not so drunk that she doesn't know what she's doing, but drunk enough to have bought a painting. She's in the Maputo airport departure area, seated on a green and chrome plastic chair, with a long orange cylinder standing to attention next to her knee. Inside it, two solemn angels turned inwards, away from the world, white wings hidden from the world.

It's an interesting experience, buying art while lubricated by two glasses of cold white wine and the companionship of an old friend. She remembers the things of beauty she has seen during her travels that she has left behind, turning her back on the expense and then unable to turn her back on the regret of opportunity lost.

She envisages the swirling silk tapestry that she left hanging on the gallery wall in Quito, the… no, hang on, is that the only piece she loved and didn't buy? Perhaps she hasn't left a trail of unattainable beauty behind. Maybe it is only that one piece. Whatever, the angels stared at her from the linocut and she knew she had to have them. Knew that she wanted their serenity to smile on her from her wall. Knew she wanted to share her house with them. Two brown-skinned angels, heads wreathed in white *doeks*, framed by white wings against a sienna landscape and a blue sky.

*You don't believe in angels*, says the devil on her shoulder.

'I don't believe in dragons, but I love them,' she snaps back. 'Don't be so mundane.' *Don't be so impulsive.*

'Why not? It's what makes the world interesting.'

*You need meaning in your life, not interesting.*

'I need this painting in my life. And it is here, in my path to the plane, and my credit card is in my hand, and the rest, as they say, is history.'

*You've had too much to drink*

'On the contrary, I've had just enough."

A glass of wine for each angel, a swipe of the card, and they are mine. Their forms were carved into a linoleum block with a sharp knife, inked, and pressed layer upon layer onto soft paper until the image was complete. And ready to travel. She knows that the wine is still oiling her synapses when she questions whether they will feel at home in her house, hopes that they will.

The artist is dead, it appears, died young, and only twenty of his angels exist in the world – ten pairs, heads wreathed in identical white *doeks*, framed against identical sienna landscapes and turquoise skies.

What could have ended his life so early, this Mabote, Shangaan of origin, trained in Mozambique, with his vision of angels? AIDS, she thinks, the most likely cause, shrinking his muscles around his bones, his skin, eating at him from the inside like rats in the dark until their teeth pierced his face, leaving black-edged wounds in his skin. And still they ate at him from the inside, until there was no muscle left to hold his bones together and he fell away into the dark with only the angels to catch him.

She's never flown with angels before, particularly not in the luggage rack above her head. It's unlikely that anyone else on the plane can feel their presence. Most people have their eyes shut already, a range or snores and sleepy grunts issuing from their noses and throats; or their eyes fixed on the screen, watching silent cyclists race along tarred streets in some unknown city.

It is Friday night and her fellow passengers are tired, the long week over, the last drops of energy sucked away by the drone of the plane. She plugs into Mozart, her own form of meditation and feels the last of the wine drain away, leaving the residue of the week's frustrations like the fur of last night's hangover on her tongue.

Ninety pages of report, handed over to the technical editor.

Ninety pages of report, handed back by the technical editor.

'Can't do it,' said the technical editor. 'There are pieces that don't make sense. And the whole thing needs to be restructured. It's a mess.'

Stella is annoyed. 'Sandile reviewed it, dammit. I asked him to edit the bloody thing. What do you mean it's a mess?'

The technical editor points to a page in front of him. Stella leans forward, peers at the page. Reads. Stops. Reads again.

'See?'

'Bloody hell. How did that get through?'

'See?'

Now her weekend is going down the tubes with ninety pages of a sub-consultant report that she'll rewrite on her own time because there's no money left in the project budget and the sub-consultant is bloody useless. Even though she's tempted to send it back to him and tell him to spend his weekend rewriting it, she knows it'll just come back amended, but not necessarily improved; she'll save herself a great deal of angst by rewriting it herself. And at least she won't wake up and wonder what to do with her day.

Much though she might not want it, she knows exactly what she'll have to do with her day. She sighs.

# Table Mountain

Stella wakes up irked. Outside the clouds are pressing against the window, the wind squeezing itself through between the closed window and the frame. A Cape Town winter day. And she is going to walk up Table Mountain.

She rolls over, pulling the duvet around her neck, trying to get a few extra minutes of warmth before she is forced out of bed and into the cold. Mark will be here any minute, international author in tow. Mark had an obligation to take the guy up Table Mountain, but she can't remember why she agreed to go with them. Some misguided notion that it might be interesting.

Old Chinese curse, she thinks, 'may you live in interesting times'. Well, Table Mountain in this weather was certainly going to be interesting. This was the weather in which they advised you *not* to go up Table Mountain. The kind of weather in which people got lost, or slipped and fell to their deaths, or at least to their broken hips.

Bugger.

Mark would be here any minute and he wasn't going to take no for an answer. She remembers how he pleaded, over a one-too-many glass of wine, for her to leaven the pressure of the company of a famous writer. Mark wasn't the small talk type. He needed her to make conversation …

She sighs, slips her feet into sheepskin slippers and shuffles through to the bathroom.

Half an hour later, her boots are laced and she climbs into the back seat of Mark's car, pushes over his day pack to make space and kicks an empty juice bottle out of the way of her feet. The car has the tense ambience of two strangers trapped in a small space and a large silence. She clears her throat.

'Morning all,' she tosses into the silence. 'Great weather!'

'It's my last day,' the author tosses over his shoulder. 'If I don't climb the mountain today, I won't be able to do it at all.'

'I know,' she smiles. 'Mark told me. Not that you'll see very much in this weather.'

'I'm Scottish,' he smiles back. 'This feels very normal.'

Mark negotiates the tight curves of Kloof Nek, taciturn and competent. He parks the car, hauls out his pack, and they start towards the bottom of India Venster and the long walk up the side of the mountain.

The Scottish writer looks up at the massif. 'Finally,' he says, 'finally I get to walk on Table Mountain.' He smiles at Stella. 'I'm writing about great rocks of the world, sacred rocks. Like Ayers Rock, and Table Mountain. This is a very special place. The Xhosa people call it Watcher of the South. When Qamata was creating the world, the sea dragon Nkanyamba tried to stop him.

'According to the legend, they had an intense battle, and Qamata's mother, the Earth Goddess, created four giants to protect the four corners of the world and to help Qamata. When Qamata had created enough land, the giants died and turned into stone to watch over the cardinal points of the earth forever. The southernmost one, who was also the biggest and strongest, was named Umlindi Wemingizimu, Watcher of the South. He is Table Mountain.'

Strange, thinks Stella, hearing a local story told to her in a thick Scottish accent. She has never heard the story before. Seems like the guy has done his homework. She grunts and sets off along the path.

India Venster is a deceptive route. It starts with a stiff walk uphill, some rock scrambling, even a small chimney, which, to Stella's annoyance, Mark has to boost her up, her arms and thighs no longer able to lift her chubby body up the narrow space. The Scottish man, by contrast, hauls himself up with wiry arms, despite his superior age.

Just above the chimney, they sit down for a cup of tea, cocooned in the mist, the rest of the world hidden from sight and sound. Stella tries not to think of the website warning not to climb India Venster in bad weather, that the route is dangerous. She focuses on the little pot, willing the water to boil, while the damp seeps through her trousers and down her neck.

Through the mist, two apparitions appear from the rock chimney. First, a middle-aged black man in a tweed jacket, brown leather shoes, and a pork-pie hat. Behind him, a woman in a white skirt, sleeveless white shirt, bare feet, and an array of white and yellow beads, steps out of the mist. Stella stares at them. Who are these people and what are they doing on the mountain in this weather?

The man steps forward, pulls his hat from his head, and greets them. 'Good morning,' he says. 'How do you do?'

'Hello,' Mark responds. 'Where are you guys going?'

'This is my sister.' He gestures to the woman who shivers in the cold. 'She is a water *sangoma*. We are going to the top of the mountain so that she can pray over the water there.'

'Have you ever been up the mountain before?' asks Mark, and concern wrinkles the skin around his eyes. Stella remembers the website warning.

'No. We came to take the cable car. But it isn't running today. Because of the weather, they said. Then we saw the sign, Table Mountain, so we are walking up. My sister needs to do this today.'

'You'd better stick with us. This is a difficult route, and quite dangerous if you don't know the way. And your sister looks like she's struggling.'

'She has been fasting for five days to be clean for this purpose. When she has prayed, she can eat again.'

Mark digs down into his bag and hauls out a spare fleece. 'Tell her to wear this.'

The woman takes the fleece without comment, slides her arms into the over-long arms and wraps it gratefully across her chest.

They pack up the empty cups, drain the last of the tea out of the pot onto the damp ground, and begin up the path again. Stella watches with concern as the sangoma sways along the path, her equilibrium unsettled by five days of fasting.

Three hours later, they clamber up the last few metres and onto the top. Flat ground at last. Stella's thighs ache, and her hands are cold, but she dare not put them into her pockets in case she slips on the damp rocks.

A couple of hundred metres in, they come to the reservoir. 'This has water in it?' the man asks. 'She must pray next to water.'

'Yes.'

The writer watches with glee as the sangoma closes her eyes and prays, a brief but fervent prayer in isiXhosa. Words over, she reaches into a pouch tied around her waist and tosses a handful of mealie seeds into the reservoir.

'Now she can eat,' says her brother, and she opens her eyes and looks around.

Hungrily, no doubt, thinks Stella.

It is at this point that Stella discovers that the only food they have is the half-eaten bar of chocolate she grabbed from the table as she left the house. I don't believe it, she thinks, Mark brought us up here with no food! What did he think – that we'd be up and down before lunch? It's taken us nearly four hours to get up here, and I'm bloody hungry! Stupid man. Why do I trust him? I know he does this. Bloody idiot. And we still have to walk all the way down because the bloody cable car isn't running. Without any food. Awesome! What a shitty day.

She hands over the chocolate to the sangoma.

They move on towards the cable car and the mist swirls around. It might not be running, but they will find a sheltered spot for another cup of tea.

While they huddle against the wind and the chilly clouds and wait for the tea to boil, Mark sets off towards the buildings near the cable car. 'Coming?' he tosses over his shoulder to Stella.

Better than staying still and getting cold, she thinks, and wanders after him wondering what he intends to do amongst these clearly deserted buildings.

Mark knocks on the first door. No reply.

And the next.

No reply.

No surprise, thinks Stella. It's all shut down because of the weather – there's no one here. But third time lucky, and the door opens to his knock, a young bearded face peers out at them.

Ismail and Jan have just cooked a huge pot of vegetarian biryani. Or rather, Ismail cooked while Jan watched the rugby. South Africa vs the British and Irish Lions. They have a heater on and the small room is toasty warm as Mark, the Scottish writer, Stella, the man in his pork-pie hat, and his sangoma sister, bundle themselves in and seat themselves on whatever flat surface avails itself. The two young men pull out plates and cutlery and dish up biryani to the hungry group.

Stella's sense of humour returns as her stomach fills, her skin loses its goose bumps and her fingers begin to regain their sense of feeling. On the screen, the guys in green push through for a try, and they all grin and clap. I don't even like rugby, Stella admits, with an inward chuckle.

The walk down Platteklip Gorge is easier than the walk up, but Stella's legs are shaky by the time they reach the bottom. It is a long time since she has done so much exercise in one day. She anticipates the pleasure of dry clothes and a cup of coffee.

The Scottish guy witters on about how fascinating it has been, waving goodbye to pork-pie and his sister as they climb into a minibus taxi. 'Remarkable,' he says, 'to find a, what do you call her, a sangoma on the sacred mountain like that.

Amazing how the universe makes these things happen for one.' Yeah, right, thinks Stella.

# The Tattooed Lady

At a plastic table in the only restaurant in international departures, behind a red plastic squeeze bottle of tomato sauce, sits a tattooed lady. Not an escapee from a circus but a middle-aged, rather overweight woman with pink highlights in her hair and a wild-haired woman in full colour emblazoned across her saggy upper arm. She's dressed in a sleeveless black and white shirt, black trousers, flat black pumps. All in all, quite ordinary, apart from the red-haired lady on her arm.

The red hair makes the tattooed lady's arm look sunburnt. Presumably not the look she was going for. Stella feels old-fashioned, left behind by the tattoo craze. Although relieved that there is no brightly coloured picture that draws attention to her cellulite. How foolish we are, she thinks, we primp and decorate ourselves like bowerbirds, in the hope of what? Love? Attention? Immortality? No that's too much. That's what religion does, not tattoos, tight dresses and lipstick.

She sips her bottled water, wills time to move faster. Her cell phone pings once like a temple bell and the tattooed woman looks up, tired bags under her eyes.

It's Sandra. 'Mum's not doing well. Would be good if you could phone her. If you can find the time.'

How can she be so snide in such a short message? thinks Stella. I'll phone when I get home. We'll board soon and it's too expensive to phone on roaming.'

But an errant thought that sneaks around somewhere between her limbic system and her prefrontal cortex bears witness that she has no intention of phoning. Drained by the idea, let alone the action, she deletes the message. Orders a glass of wine, knows that it will be cheap and sharp, made bearable only by a lot of ice. She sighs. Wishes she was in her own lounge with a glass of Inverroche.

The tattooed woman rises and strides past Stella, blazing lady trembling with every step. Stella's head snaps around.

It can't be, but, dear god, it is.

The blazing lady cuddles a cattle skull, and on the ground, between her kneeling legs, is a pool of blood. It can only be menstrual blood. This woman walks around with a menstruating woman with long red hair on her arm.

What the hell is that about? Stella feels very old. And conservative. And a tad shocked. She seems to have lost her grip on the world around her. She takes a large gulp of wine that is only millimetres away from being vinegar. The taste seems appropriate. She shivers.

# He's Dead

Stella stares at the newspaper obituary, her hands shake and her heart beats out a drum roll that she's sure they can hear down the passage. He's older, hair white, glasses more modern than back then, but it is unmistakably him. Advocate Smiley Theron. It's true, he did smile a lot, including the first time he slid his hand across her thigh at the table in the dining room where he helped her with her Afrikaans essay – her parents' idea of how to improve her poor marks.

Smiley Theron, Dad's good friend, her Afrikaans tutor. She was shocked, delighted, a fourteen-year-old who wanted affirmation, feeling the first stirrings of sexual desire. What she wanted, she now knows after years of therapy, was her father's love. The first time it was only that, he rested his hand on her thigh while they discussed the use of the double negative, colloquial and formal.

Funny how she can remember both with such clarity. Perhaps sexual stimulation and fear heighten brain activity. She remembers the moment as if in slow motion. She was terrified, almost horrified, at least in part by her desire for his hand to move further. She remembers how the heat flooded through her body, how difficult it was to concentrate. What was he doing? What should she do? He was her father's closest friend, he would never do something wrong. This must be OK. Why then did she feel so confused? She was shamed by her desire, kept awake at night by it.

It was a slow progression, week by week. He brought her presents –a bottle of perfume, fancy hand cream, expensive chocolates. Told her not to tell her parents, that it was his gift to her for her hard work. Told her that good marks were all her parents needed to see.

He wooed her with tenderness and care. She fell in love.

He was older, wiser, kind and patient. She waited for their weekly lessons with the anticipation of a junkie waiting for a fix. She worked late at night on her Afrikaans to see him smile at her improvement. Her marks soared. Her parents were delighted. Smiley was such a good tutor, they said. What a good idea it was to bring him in. And Smiley smiled and nodded.

And Stella wondered why her parents couldn't see what was going on, torn between the hope that they would intervene and the passionate desire that they wouldn't.

Over months, his hand moved up her thigh, closer to the ache between her legs. Day by day, desire conquered shame and she felt her thighs move apart, begging his fingers to move deeper. The first time he touched her 'there' – she had no name for her clitoris in those days – she knew this was all she wanted, to be with this man forever, feeling this ecstasy.

'Don't tell your parents,' he whispered, 'let this be our secret.'

And she nodded, loved the complicity that bound them together. Secret love. Forever. It carried a mystique. Not like statutory rape. She didn't know those words then. She was in love. Thought he was too.

She never told her parents. Not even when he told her it had to stop, told her that he still loved her, but his wife was suspicious.

'Leave her,' Stella said with the naïve passion of a fifteen-year-old. 'Leave her and we can be together.' She hated his wife, the elegant doctor who shared his bed, who had borne him children about her age.

'It's not that easy,' he responded, sterner than he had ever been. 'I have children with her, I have a job. You and I can't be together. People won't understand. I could go to jail. You don't want that, do you?' He caressed her breasts as he spoke, slid his hand between her legs, pulled her hand onto his tumescent penis.

'One last time,' he whispered and pulled her towards him. 'You'll get over me,' he said, 'you'll find a nice boy your own age.' And then he smiled his secret smile and left.

I don't want a boy my own age, she screamed, in silence, I want you. She turned and wept into the pink roses on her pillows.

He went back to his wife and his two blonde children and his perfect life and she fell into a rabbit hole, down and down like Alice. Her parents didn't understand what had happened, why her marks suddenly dropped, why she no longer studied, why she cried so much.

'Boyfriend trouble?' asked her mother, and Stella felt a wave of panic that her mother might know. She nodded but said nothing more. 'Sorry sweetie,' said her mother. 'But you're young, it'll pass. Just concentrate on your schoolwork and forget about him. Go out with your friends. You'll find someone else soon enough. There are lots of lovely boys out there. Nice boys your age.'

But she hasn't really, thinks Stella. She's had relationships, but she's never found the one person that others seem to find, the one relationship that lasts through thick and thin, the lifetime friend and lover. She blames Smiley.

So does her therapist.

And now he's dead. At long last, he's dead. But it is too late. His death means nothing to Stella now, the damage done long ago. She pushes the paper aside and turns back to her computer, her fingers shake as she opens the draft report from Peter and begins to read.

# Thief Again

Bloody hell. It's happened again. Someone has nicked the petty cash again – sometime between Friday lunchtime (when the office lunch was paid for) and Monday morning when Fezile prepared to reconcile the slips. Fifteen hundred Rand gone. Fezile is sitting in Sleazy Nick's office again, looking shocked and scared.

When the hell is she going to get angry instead, wonders Stella.

This time it was different though. Sleazy Nick had been clever for once – he'd come in over a weekend when no one was around and installed a camera that stared down with an unblinking electronic eye at the petty cash drawer, cleverly disguised as an alarm beam thingy.

Clever, she thought, and wondered whether the blackout over the weekend would have interfered with it. I bet he didn't think of that, she thought a little with glee, that the guys who dug up the pavement would put a backactor through the power cables and plunge us into three days of darkness. It would be bitter irony if the thief weren't caught because of some idiot workmen with an oversized mechanised spade.

She scratches distractedly at an itchy nipple, then glances at the alarm beam thingy in the corner of her room. Is that really an alarm beam thingy? How long has it been there, or has Sleazy Nick put up cameras all over the place? She relaxes. Nick is too tight with money to put up more cameras than needed. She scratches again at the offending nipple.

She wonders who Sleazy Nick will see on the screen – does he already have his suspicions, or will it be a rude surprise to him and to others? She wonders how he will handle it when he's seen the video (or the stills – why did she assume it was video? Too many movies?).

Would someone just not come back to work the next day? Would he announce it to the whole staff, call them into the boardroom –all of them except one, since you couldn't announce in front someone that they were being thrown out for petty theft. She presumes that stealing petty cash is, by definition, petty theft? Not grand larceny.

It happened between Friday lunch and Monday morning, again. Only three people come to mind as having had the opportunity over that timeframe.

Of the three, she hopes it's Phola. Not that she dislikes her, but Alice can't afford to lose her job, and Zara, well, Zara is a spoiled little rich girl, but she has an acerbic sense of humour that Stella enjoys. And if Zara goes, Stella will be in real trouble on the AfDB report – she'll struggle to pull it together without Zara's economic expertise. And it will be a challenge to find a good economist to replace her at this stage.

Bugger, thinks Stella. Not Zara. Please, not Zara.

Whoa, she thinks, not so quick – anyone could have stolen the cash – everyone in the office has a key, knows the alarm code. Anyone could have come in over the weekend and nicked it. That makes her shudder – that makes it less opportunistic, more pre-meditated.

Does that make it worse? Theft is theft, isn't it? And no, of course it isn't that simple – some people steal out of need, because they're hungry, or can't pay the school bills. Others steal – well, because they can, she thinks, and because they got away with it the first time and it seems easier the second time. Scientists have proved that lying gets easier with the more lies you tell – does the same apply to stealing? Presumably.

Whoever did it has grown in confidence. It's over 3000 Rand in a matter of a few weeks. Or perhaps the person has grown desperate. That would somehow feel better. To know that someone needed the money would make it easier than someone who just took it for a little bit extra. Or to feed a habit.

She turns back to the AfDB report, but her mind wanders, she wonders if the thief knows the net is closing in. If she knows that Nick installed a camera then pretty much everyone in the office must, the thief included, whose senses must be particularly attuned to any changes in office behaviour. What is going through the mind of the thief? Is s/he scared, remorseful, riddled with guilt, or does s/he have a ready explanation to justify the theft? She read that creative people have the most highly developed ability to lie to themselves. In that case, she thought, there are a lot of people out there with deeply hidden creative talents.

She thinks back to a murder case that most of the country listened to through daily live court proceedings on the radio. People started to drop phrases like 'I put it to you…' and 'dolus eventualis' into their tea-time chats – a nation of overnight legal experts.

What Stella wanted to know was whether the accused had convinced himself that his unlikely defence was true, or if he knew that he was lying to the court, to the country, and to himself. 'I thought it was a burglar.'

In your toilet? Behind a locked door? And you didn't check where your girlfriend was before you pulled the trigger? You shot her, you bastard, she thought, shot her in a testosterone-and-steroid-fuelled rage, through a closed door into a tiny toilet cubicle. You knew she was in there and you pulled the trigger four times. Four times. With black talon bullets designed to rip through human flesh in the most destructive way possible. Bullets designed to kill. That's murder. That's femicide. That's another blip in the great global rage against women.

Get a grip, she thinks. It was just some petty cash. And she opens up the AfDB report. 'Pick up where you left off,' her computer offers, and she sighs and complies.

# Conflict Avoidance

Stella is sad. Marrow-bone sad and anxious. She feels it like a grey fog in her brain and the pressure of tears around her eyes. Not even the white-bellied sunbird on the luminous orange flowers of the Aloe ferox cheer her up. She knows this emotion, knows the desire to run and hide that comes with it, knows now where it comes from. Doesn't know how to still it, though, to let it go.

Tomorrow she has to meet with the client on the Lesotho project, Mr Thamae, a short, intense man who wants more from her than he can pay for. She knows it will be tough, remembers the last meeting in which his bullying tactics forced her to work long, unbillable hours to finish work that he had demanded, but that was not in the contract. She knows, in her marrow, that he will do it again, thinks she even knows what it is that he will ask for.

And she knows that she will have to refuse. They are right up against the budget, no wiggle room, and she's damned if she is going to put more free work in just to placate him.

But a small, sad part of her brain is already formulating the arguments as to why she should, perhaps, do it, how she can squeeze it in over a weekend, how perhaps it can be justified if you interpret the terms of reference rather generously. She watches that corner of her brain with mild contempt, seeing the conflict-averse peacemaker raise its pathetic head and try to find a way out.

'You need to learn to set stronger boundaries,' her shrink used to say, in the days before she grew tired of her tears about herself, and her pain, and her dreadful, comfortable, middleclass life. 'You need to be more convinced that it is OK to set boundaries and what those boundaries are. You come across so strong, but internally your boundaries are porous, like our border with Zim. And just like the government, you let people through and through and through until one day you've had enough and you lash out. And then the people around you are confused because they don't know what they did wrong …

'You know only too well what happens when you aren't true to your personal values, when you don't set clear boundaries.'

Oh yes, I know, thinks Stella, picturing her childhood and her mother's lack of boundaries. I wonder where I got it from!

'Don't you dare speak to me like that,' her mother would spit at her, 'don't you dare disrespect me like that. You are an ungrateful little girl. You can't go to Susan's place tonight if you are going to treat me like that. And those shoes you wanted, you can't have those either.'

'But you promised.'

'Well, I changed my mind. Tough luck.'

'But Mum—'

'Don't "but mum" me …'

And then the tears, from both of them, and the hugs, and I'm sorry, and a new pair of shoes and presented as triumphant evidence of love.

'But I wanted the blue ones.'

'Don't be ungrateful. These are beautiful, much prettier than the blue ones.'

She wanted the blue shoes, the right to choose, a stable world where the rules didn't change from day-to-day. A world without the electric fences of what was or was not and which ran concealed through the dark corridors of her mother's mind.

'Know your priorities,' her shrink would have said. 'Be measured, steady, consistent, don't get caught up in the drama. Try to find a win-win solution, and if that doesn't work, stand your ground, quietly, but firmly.'

Fine words when the tears prick at your eyes and your hands start to shake and an ancient tsunami of not being good enough threatens to sweep away your mask of professionalism and leave you pudding-faced – blancmange pudding – wobbling at the slightest bump.

Oh, fuck it. Why does it rise up again and again, this sense of worthlessness? Will she ever get past it? Liberated into the world of other people who seem to feel just fine, who don't carry Smiley Therons and roller-coaster mothers in their baggage. How is she going to handle Mr Thamae without taking on a pile of extra work? And without pissing him off. She needs to think it through, plan out a strategy, but the fog in her brain makes her eyelids heavy and she wants to curl up in her bed with *Downton Abbey* and forget all about it.

Until she wakes up in the morning, with her stomach cramped with anxiety.

Maybe a gin will help. A stiff gin. With one ice and lemon. Her mother would say it was too early in the day for a drink. The sun not yet over the yardarm. Whatever a fucking yardarm is. But then her mother didn't have to deal with Mr fucking Thamae and his endless demands.

The white-bellied sunbird flits up and down the flower spike, drinks his fill, while his drab wife nips in and out of the *bloubos*, onto the aloe spike and back, shyly, into the bloubos. Stella feels the gin run down her throat and into her veins. Dutch courage.

Bit rough on the Dutch, she thinks, to assume they needed a slug of grog to feel brave. But then, who the hell would want to rush onto a battlefield stone-cold sober?

Mr Thamae looks at her oddly. Or so it feels. She wishes now that she hadn't gulped down the Dutch courage, that she had entered the battlefield stone-cold sober. She's sure he can't smell it, but she struggles to read the room, worried that she's a bit loud, a bit aggressive. But fuck it, what does he really want from this project?

'Rre Thamae,' she says, using the polite title, 'I understand what you are asking for, but I don't think that was part of the original terms of reference, and we really don't have the budget to include any extra work.'

Did she just say that, straight out, to the monstrous Mr Thamae? Must be the gin talking, she thought.

'Mme,' he responds, the polite title masks a voice as thick as a coiled puff adder, 'Mme, the terms of reference call for a regulatory impact assessment. That's all I am asking for.'

'Yes, Rre, the ToR ask for an RIA. But as we put in our proposal, and as we agreed in our inception meeting, the RIA would be a high-level qualitative one. Not quantified. Now you want me to quantify the impacts. We don't have the data to do that. We'd have to do primary research for that. And that wasn't included in the budget or in the inception report.'

'What use to us is an RIA that isn't quantified?'

The puff adder tenses. She can sense its venom. Why does this man hate her so much? She's tired. The Dutch courage has ebbed, the early start has caught up with her, and she feels like a mouse. And then the mouse morphs. A gin-fuelled mongoose rears up on its hind legs and pounces. And the mongoose always wins.

'Rre,' she tries to remain polite, 'Rre, on page thirteen of the inception report, we clearly stated, "The regulatory impact assessment will be a high-level RIA that addresses the issues from a qualitative perspective only. The economic impacts of the project will not be quantified. Should this be required an additional budget will be required to complete this piece of work".'

'That's not …' he interrupts, politeness dropped.

'You approved the inception report at the meeting on the 17th January. I have the minutes here. You approved the minutes at the meeting on the 23rd March.'

The puff adder is bewildered. The mongoose moves too fast.

'If you have comments on the RIA as we agreed that it would be produced, as a qualitative document, then I would love to hear them so that we can address them.'

The mongoose relaxes, sways from side to side, watches its prey, waits for an opening.

'I will send through my comments in writing,' the puff adder mumbles.

Bloody hell, the mongoose thinks, he didn't even read it. She's enjoying this.

'That would be excellent,' she smiles, sharp teeth only slightly bared. 'When can we expect your comments? Can we have them by the end of the week? I'd like to finalise the report and get it back to you as soon as possible.'

'Monday.' The puff adder has shrunk like a burst condom. A harmless house snake curls in its place. 'I'll send you my comments on Monday.'

'Excellent,' smiles Stella. 'Can we talk about the implementation plan?'

The flight back is short but joyous. She is energised and awake. She squeezes her computer into the tiny space between her and the seat in front, and, elbows tucked in against her ribs, she starts to type.

# Alice

It's official. Alice the Light-Fingered stole the money and has gone, shunted without ceremony out of the office and into the midst of the great unemployed, eight-year-old child in tow. How the hell is she going to feed him now, wonders Stella. And the violent boyfriend? She's seen the bruises on Alice's skin under the thick make-up. How long will he stay now that her income has dried up? What a mess, she thinks.

# Attack of the Killer Calamari

The right side of her body feels absent in the most peculiar way. It's taken her at least a minute to type a sentence. The fingers of her right hand, used to racing across the keyboard like Usain Bolt on steroids, seem to have forgotten everything they knew, and she must search for each letter, peck at the keyboard like a *hadeda* on the lawn. Her left hand, unaffected, skitters along. Together her hands scramble the words into dyslexia.

She's alone and very scared.

At three in the morning, yesterday's calamari rose up against her and pitched towards the toilet, belly clutched against the cramps. She hugged the rubbish bin to her chest for the vomit while her stomach heaved and hurled diarrhoea into the toilet bowl with the power of a Ferrari. In the midst of which a dark rush of pain started from the base of her neck and swept up into her brain.

She would have sobbed if there had been any space left in her wracked body for tears. Her stomach rejected the painkillers in a violent spasm, and she spent a pathetic night alternately clutching her head and stumbling to the toilet.

In the morning, when she'd walked through to the kitchen to get juice, she seemed to have lost the right side of her body. As if it was no longer there. She'd slammed her right shoulder into the Oregon pine doorframe. She poured juice to rehydrate her jaded body with her left hand, as if her right had been amputated. She'd looked down, surprised to see it still there.

And now she can't type. Dear god, she thinks in panic, was that pain a stroke? Is that what happened? Using only her left hand, and fighting back notions of mortality, she Googles 'what does a stroke feel like'?

Severe headache that comes on for no reason.

Oh shit.

Blurred vision, trouble speaking.

Don't have those.

Weakness on one side of the body.

Oh shit.

She leaves a message for Dr Linde.

It is at least an hour of angst before she returns the call in a snatched moment between one emergency and another. 'Typhoid,' she gabbles, 'sweeping down from Zimbabwe, seen lots of it. I'll email a script for antibiotics.'

'I can't type. My right hand doesn't work.'

'This bug produces neurotoxins.'

Neurotoxins? The word conjures up African savannahs, black mambas and instant death. Stella is not consoled but Dr Linde has no time for reassurance. Stella sits with the phone still to her ear, seized with panic about whether she will ever type again and whether voice recognition software has progressed far enough that she can still work if she can't type. She would cry, but she is dehydrated and depleted and no tears come.

Her good hand clenches in dread. Oh my god. What if it's one of those parasites that takes over your brain to further its own ends. She's read about it in rats. *Toxoplasma gondii*. It's designed to live in cats. If, by some strange error, it ends up in a rat, it seeps into the rat's brain and modifies it. It eradicates the rat's fear of cats. In fact, it makes the rat attracted to cats. Rat ventures near cat, cat eats rat, *gondii* ends up back in cat.

Stella Googles *toxoplasma gondii* in humans. For a moment, she goes cold before she starts to laugh. *Gondii in* humans makes women warmer and friendlier. Despite feeling that her head might explode and that her neck has been run over by a jumbo jet, Stella is amused.

Not likely that I've been infected then, she thinks.

By Sunday morning, she has barely eaten for three days. Her broken body craves papaya, so she hops into her car, headachy and nauseous, and heads for the supermarket. The drive is terrifying. The steering wheel feels disconnected from the car. She turns right, almost mounts the pavement. Her spatial orientation is badly awry. She concentrates fiercely on the road, but the car handles as if the tires are flat. She is exhausted and shaken by the time she gets back home. She drops the papaya on the table in the entrance hall and collapses onto her bed.

The next morning, when she wakes up still with a severe headache and nausea, Stella heads for the Milpark Hospital by Uber. It is Monday morning, and Outpatients is eerily empty. After a short while, she is seen by a young doctor who whisks her off for a scan. She's too tired to feel claustrophobic in the MRI tunnel, and gives herself willingly into the arms of the great god of technology, in the hope of a cure.

A while later, she has no idea how long, she finds herself in the outpatient ward, on a white bed surrounded by white curtains. The doctor appears through the curtains. She smiles at him.

'So, doctor, am I going to die today or tomorrow?' His shocked look stops her in her tracks. Her smile fades.

'Well, no. But I do have some bad news for you. You have a cerebral haemorrhage.' All sound stops. The moment hangs frozen in space and time. 'It's a small bleed, but we're going to have to admit you. They might need to operate.'

She struggles to locate herself in this frightening reality. The one in which there is damage to her brain. The one in which she is no longer bulletproof. Panic coats her throat.

'I'll get someone to come and book you in, and then we'll do some more tests. That way they'll come off your hospital plan, not your medical savings.'

And then she is alone in a white bed behind a white curtain with her dysfunctional arm, her bleeding brain and her fear.

The rest of the day is a blur of forms and scans, culminated in being wheeled into the ICU to wait for the neurosurgeon. She hasn't eaten, but no one can tell her whether she's allowed to eat or not. The threat of emergency surgery hangs in the air like the sword of Damocles.

Who was Damocles anyway?

She has nothing to read. Nothing to do. Across the room, an oversized piece of medical equipment mocks her with its name: Mindray. She can't conceive what it might be. She stares at the pictures on the silent TV and drifts off into a restless sleep.

Family members huddle around the still shape of the old woman in the next bed when she surfaces. Their voices are hushed, their heads bowed under the weight of imminent death. At the end of the ward, a woman calls out in delirium, meaningless syllables of pain and confusion. The sister shushes her sharply. Across from her, a woman lies motionless on a ventilator while dialysis keeps a middle-aged man alive.

'Drank my liver into extinction,' he says.

Great company, she thinks.

It is late in the evening when Dr Tsela arrives. He stands at the foot of her bed, scan in one hand. He seems absurdly young and self-confident. Stella is not sure whether to be reassured or unnerved by his cockiness. She chooses to believe in him. She needs to believe in him.

'Small bleed in the left temporal lobe,' she hears him say. 'It looks like the bleeding has stopped, but we'd like to keep you in to be perfectly sure.'

'Do you need to operate?' She sounds pathetic to her own ears.

'Doesn't look like it. We'll keep watching you, but I think the worst is over.'

She is flooded with relief. She dreaded the idea that someone might poke around in her brain with sharp instruments. She has watched too much *Grey's Anatomy*. She sniggers.

Dr Tsela vanishes with a cheery wave and a flirtatious comment in isiZulu to the nurse who giggles and leaves, to return with jelly and custard. It hasn't changed since she had her tonsils out forty-five years ago. She smiles at the familiar taste and sinks back into the pillows. She is excruciatingly tired.

The next two days slide around her in a blur of blood tests and scans and sleep, interspersed with TV and visits from friends. She feels like a pincushion from the needles that have been stuck into her. But she sleeps with a strange comfort, knows people are tending to her. She hasn't felt so cared for in a long time.

On the evening of day two, Dr Tsela returns to her bedside, waves her latest iodine contrast scan.

'You're fine,' he states with a proud smile as if he had cured her. 'There is no underlying weakness. It was a once-off event, and it has long since stopped bleeding. You can go home.' She stares at him. The words don't make sense.

'I'm discharging you, you can go home.' He smiles his most winning smile.

'Now?'

'Now.' She is bewildered, she did not expect to be ejected from her cocoon at 8:30 at night. The nurse too looks confused.

'Off you go,' he states, signs a prescription with a swirl of his expensive pen and hands it to her.

And so, de-needled, de-robed and clutching a packet full of painkillers and anti-inflammatories, she staggers into an Uber and into two weeks of sick leave.

Ten days later Simon, an old colleague who now lives in London, Skypes her.

'I hear you had a stroke? Are you OK?'

How the hell did you hear that? The grapevine has long tendrils.

'I'm fine,' she replies. 'It was just a small cerebral haemorrhage. No lasting damage.' Liar, she thinks. Dr Tsela said your chance of an epileptic seizure has just trebled.

'Wow,' responds Steven with a smiley emoticon, 'You are incredibly lucky. I have a cousin who had a stroke a couple of months ago. The left side of her body is virtually useless. She can barely speak.'

I hate emoticons, thinks Stella, and all those who use them as some idiotic communication shortcut, but she replies, 'I have a guardian angel!'

She wakes up from a snooze – she seems to sleep a lot, gropes blearily for her computer and Googles 'stroke'. She's avoided thinking about it, but indeed, she had a haemorrhagic stroke – a bleed in the brain. She reads on, with mounting concern. Only fifteen percent of strokes are haemorrhagic – most strokes are the result of a blocked blood vessel, not a bleed. But forty percent of stroke deaths are from haemorrhagic strokes. She feels a *klap* of adrenaline.

I could have died, she thinks. I might be alive with severe brain damage, unable to walk, to drive, to talk. Unable to work.

I am mortal, she thinks. And it is not a good thought.

# Beethoven

Beethoven's 4th Piano Concerto. A small orchestra, a full house, and an emaciated creature in a tail coat who tightens the knob on the piano stool before he flicks out his tails and sits. A moment of anticipation and the first notes drop into the silence of three hundred people who wait to be pleased.

The skinny man with the long fingers tickles the key of the piano as one would the soft belly of a cat. It's not a piece she knows well. She finds it rather more sparse than the Beethoven she knows, shot through with almost modern moments of discord.

She waits for the music to take her, to lift her from her seat and whirl her into another dimension, but it doesn't. She finds herself, instead, engaged intellectually by the music, fascinated by instrumental sequencing – when the clarinet comes in, how the single wind instrument pushes back against the powerful strings.

Stella watches, entertained, as the kettledrum rolls like gentle thunder, and ponders whether it is obligatory for female kettledrum players to be a little overweight, a little frumpy, against the slender-armed, silk-scarf draped elegance of the violinists. And as for the first cello, with the pointy shoes and the ferret on his head, she imagines he thinks he's funky, hip, with-it, but he's missed his sell-by date and his look is as sadly passé as his sagging jowls.

The pianist is off again, fingers race across the keys, hand over hand, and back again, his face stern. After the ascetism of the fourth, the fifth throws its thumping, beer-drinking rhythm across the hall. Her head starts to rock, her feet tap, her hands wave in her lap. She hasn't been lifted from her seat and transported away, but there is something visceral about the fifth. She is flooded with gratitude that she is alive. That she still has a functional head to rock to music.

A hand falls on her shoulder. She turns, surprised, follows the hand up a sleeve jacket to the face above it. The face frowns. Shakes its head. She raises a questioning eyebrow. The tight mouth hisses, 'Stop moving your head.'

She turns back to the orchestra, chastised, constrains herself and feels her enjoyment repressed. She glances around. Everyone is completely still.

Bloody hell. Why is classical music so formal, so draped in black dresses and black ties and so don't-rustle-your-sweet-papers, or feel it in your body? I feel good music in my body, she thinks, why am I not allowed to express it? How can these people sit so motionless when this glorious music calls their bodies to respond?

She bites her lip and compels her head to stay at least nearly still, her finger movements to shrink to micro twitches. It interferes with her enjoyment. Part of her wants to ignore the man with the hand but the stillness around her is oppressive. They could be carved in stone, and they send stone vibes in her direction. So, she turns to stone – well, maybe stone during a minor earth tremor – and tries to listen inside her head instead of with her body.

The second movement starts, with the sad sound of wind in willow trees on an overcast winter day. Strings, wind and silence paint the canvas. Then the piano steps in, note-by-note, draws gentle colour onto the grey landscape, and she holds her breath, feels each note, each combination of notes, each rise and fall. She remembers that music activates the same reward systems in the brain as addictive drugs, food and sex.

Beethoven, she thinks, much less complicated than sex and just as good. So much easier to change tracks. And she nearly snorts aloud, just in time remembering the stone bodies around her with their hyper-vigilant ears. She swallows the snort and listens to the gentle song of the piano on a bed of strings.

# Ahmed Mahfouz

It was seven and a half hours to Dubai. Three hours and forty-five minutes in the crammed business lounge. All that is left is four hours fifteen minutes to Dhaka and the Dhaka traffic before the cool black and white interior of Le Meridien, a shower, and a vast bed with crisp sheets. Most of the sixteen hours in suspended animation between here and there has passed. Stella leans back against the business class seat and relaxes.

Her reverie is disturbed by a man who settles into the seat next to her. He smiles, and she responds, polite, despite the niggle in her brain that wants him to go away, to leave her in her isolation.

'I'm Ahmed,' he says, holds out his hand. 'Ahmed Mahfouz. Pleased to meet you.'

'Stella,' she responds. As she takes his hand she hopes he isn't going to chat for the next four hours and fifteen minutes. He tells her that he is Egyptian-born, head of a transnational import-export business, and on his way to Dhaka to meet with branch management. She learns that he travels extensively, lives in Dubai, and has a wife that he seldom sees and three children, all grown up and left home.

He's charming, intelligent, and interested in her, and without noticing, she tells him the name of her hotel, how long she will be in Dhaka, that she is single and childless.

He smiles and presses her hand as they disembark and go their separate ways. She climbs into a taxi, and they wend their way through the chaotic traffic, between the knotted and draped electricity lines, the masses of people, tuk-tuks, and buses, pushing and weaving in a riot of colour and noise. They ease past shacks and hole-in-the-wall shops, past an ancient temple, pavements lined with beggars, glittering shopfronts and skyscrapers, and finally, to the doors of Le Meridien, the welcoming hands of porters and concierges, and a refreshing glass of ice-cold pineapple juice with mint.

The room is vast, the view over the bustling city marred only by the haze of pollution. She stands in the shower, washes away the flight, the stress, the grime of travel. She feels relaxed and refreshed. She orders a Bengali chicken curry and settles down in the armchair with the documents for tomorrow's meeting.

Hours later, as the sun begins to sink behind the city, gentling its noise and grunge into shades of orange and pink, the phone rings.

'Hello, ma'am. Mr Mahfouz, he is here for you.'

'Sorry, what did you say?'

'Mr Mahfouz, he is here for you. He is waiting in the lobby.'

A pulse kicks in her throat. Ahmed is here? To see her? She is surprised, grateful.

'Tell him I'm coming down.' She changes into black trousers and a soft white shirt, touches up her lipstick, brushes her hair, and applies a dab of rose perfume on her wrists and her throat.

He smiles and stands as she walks towards him. 'This is a pleasant surprise.'

'I just had to see you again,' he smiles, and she is lonely enough to forget his wife, and to smile back, just the hint of flirtation in her eyes.

'Can I get you a drink?'

'Gin and tonic, please.' He orders a double for her, a whisky for himself, and leans back, his eyes locked on hers.

They talk, about her work, his work, the state of the world, the weather in Dhaka. They have another round. They talk some more. He is attentive, interested in what she has to say. She relaxes into the conversation, but the clock is ticking.

'I must do some work,' she says. 'It has been lovely, but you must excuse me now.'

'What a pity,' he says. 'May I escort you to your room?'

At the door of her room, as she turns to say goodbye, he kisses her. It is not a goodbye kiss and her body arches into his.

Damn the work, she thinks, and opens the door.

Later that evening he kisses her on the cheek, whispers, 'You are beautiful,' draws his hand lightly across her breasts, slips back into his suit and out of the door. She lies, satiated, tangled in 400-thread count percale cotton sheets.


She wakes to the memory of his hands on her breasts, between her legs, and she shudders, torn between pleasure and shock.

What the hell was that all about, she wonders? I just got picked up on a plane and brought a strange man into my hotel room for a night of nipple-tingling sex. I'm nearly sixty, for god's sake. 'You are beautiful,' she hears again. What the hell was that all about?

Throughout her meeting, part of her brain watches her in surprise and her breasts tighten every so often with the memory of the previous night. She's sure the smell of sex must leak through her pores, but no one seems to notice, so she renews her focus on the issue at hand, something to do with building climate change response capacity at the grassroots level in Bangladesh. Sea level rise will decimate Bangladesh, she thinks. It'll need more than capacity building to cope with that.

Back at the hotel, tired from the long meeting and the grinding chaos of Dhaka traffic, a message waits for her: 'Seven o'clock in the Olea? I missed you. A.' Her hands tremble as she stuffs the note into her handbag and heads for the lift.

At 6:55, she is seated in front of the mirror; the music channel fills the room with Vivaldi. She remembers the sound of Ahmed's voice, the touch of his lips. She paints a layer of rich red lipstick to her own lips, overlaid it with the vanilla scented gloss she picked up in an airport chemist. Her lips glow back at her from the mirror. Her hair forms an elegant silver frame around her face.

Not bad, she thinks, despite the chubby neck, the bags under the sad eyes.

Why is he interested? What does he see in me?

At 6:58, she takes off the deep blue lapis lazuli earrings and hooks in the Ethiopian amber instead.

At 7:03, she brushes her hair again.

At 7:12, her phone beeps. *I am at Olea. Looking forward to being with you soon.* She stares at the message, feels a faint rise of panic. What is she doing?

At 7:15, she pulls a tissue out of her bag and, with a sense of dejection, wipes the lipstick and takes off the earrings. She turns her phone onto silent and the TV onto *The Return of the Dark Knight.*

'You wanna know how I got these scars?' Heath Ledger's disintegrated face jeers at her from the screen. The smiley evil man.

'We all carry scars,' she mutters and flips to CNN where scenes of devastation in Aleppo play across the screen. 'Oh for god's sake,' she snaps. 'There must be something to watch.'

She opens the bar fridge under the TV and pours herself a double gin with lemonade, there being no tonic. It tastes only slightly less ghastly than neat gin, but she knocks it back, pours herself a second one, settles back onto the pillows and opens her emails.

Do you want hot sex the first email asks? A sexy man will keep a lonely woman company. I am a strong and well-shaped man. Ready for the hottest sex? Then find my questionnaire attached.

She hits delete. Gulps at her gin.

At 7:23, her phone vibrates. And then again. She ignores it.

# Dying with Dignity

They emerge from bucolic Swiss meadows and hedgerows, and neat houses along the streets, into an industrial area where square-edged factories dominate the scattered fast-food joints that feed the workers. A double-storey block rises behind a trimmed hedge. The dreary late-autumn sky paints the blue metal walls with cold, and Stella shivers. Is this where this is going to take place? She'd expected something homelier, more reassuring.

She steps out of the hired car and heaves a deep breath of cold air into her lungs. She is exhausted. She needs a drink. She needs to run like hell. Instead, she grabs their handbags from the boot where her mother had insisted they be stowed, while Sandra helps their now fragile mother out of the car.

The three of them shuffle, weighed down by emotion and illness, along a wooden deck over a fishpond where goldfish swim in mindless swirls. Stella is amazed that they survive the freezing winters.

Poor bloody fish, she thinks, exported all over the world to make people feel happy, despite the weather. Her mood is as grey as the sky, and not getting any better.

They step through the door into a light, warm room with a hospital bed in on one side and a large floral-covered sofa on the other. A box of tissues is open on the table and a chubby cherub perches on a bookcase.

Great, thinks Stella, a place of tears. I so don't want to be here, sharing tears with my mother and sister.

It is five to eleven. They have been told to be here at eleven, which in Switzerland, unlike South Africa, actually means eleven.

At precisely eleven, a middle-aged woman, accompanied by a man in his thirties, walks into the room. They smile, introduce themselves, Hein and Suzette, and invite Stella, Sandra and their mother to sit at a table swathed in a bright yellow tablecloth. Stella strokes the tablecloth. She is trapped in a dream within a dream and only the tablecloth prevents her from drifting away into yet another dreamscape. Dream escape.

She signs when they put papers in front of her, nods when they want her to nod, but she knows that none of this is real, that she will wake up at her desk with an unfinished report glaring at her from the screen.

'I'm ready for the first lot,' smiles her mother with a calmness that makes Stella want to hurl the table at the lemon-coloured wall and scream into the heavy clouds overhead. There's half an hour between the antiemetic and the final dose.

Half an hour. She has a lifetime to talk about, a lifetime of sorries to utter and hear, a lifetime of love to find. Her world closes down like a dark tunnel until all she can see is the fine wrinkles on her mother's manicured hands on the yellow tablecloth, the veins in sharp relief from the shrunken flesh, the diamond ring loose now.

One of the hands moves out of her tunnel vision. She feels its cool touch on her arm.

'Are you all right, dear?'

Stupid fucking question. Of course I'm not all right. I'm fifty-fucking-eight years old and I still haven't resolved my mother issues. You were never there for me. You barely saw me or heard me. And now I have to fucking sit here and watch you take yourself away from me again. Just like always. When the going gets rough, you vanish. This time forever.

She smiles at where she thinks her mother's face must be and nods. There are no words.

'I think you'd better get me into the bed now.'

They die in the bed, thinks Stella, so that they don't slump face first onto the table. If they're in the bed they just close their eyes and go away. She shakes her head and takes a deep, shuddering breath. The tunnel cracks and light floods back. Sandra and Hein are helping her mother onto the bed while Suzette puts her shoes tidily to one side.

'Stella, can you put on the Telemann, please.' The liquid notes of Heinz Hollinger drop into the room, swell to fill the space. Her mother looks almost radiant as she holds out a hand to each of her daughters.

Stella looks at Sandra in amazement. She seems calm, even serene. Just like their mother. How is she the only one torn apart by this? She feels the light, dry fingers intertwine with hers.

'I love you, my dear. I'm sorry if I wasn't a very good mother to you. I tried my best, but you were a difficult child. I never knew how to reach you.'

Oh great, so now it's my fault?

'Sandra, you were always an easy child. I knew you'd be happy in life. I love you both. Differently. And it's been a good life. Thank you for being here with me. It means everything to me. Give me a kiss.'

Sandra leans forward and hugs her mother as if she will never let go. Stella can only stare at the hand she holds, unable to move.

'I love you both, my dearest daughters,' her mother whispers.

Too little, too late.

Her hand disengages from Stella's. Reaches out to take a tiny glass. Stella's vision is locked onto the glass. Her eyes follow it as it moves. Lips move into her field of vision. Open. The glass tilts, clear liquid trickles between the lips. A hand lowers the glass, but her eyes are imprisoned by the lips. Dry, a little cracked, lipstick smudged over the edge and leaking into the creases. The lips curve into what could be a smile.

The poisoned chalice, thinks Stella. This is goodbye.

Suzette takes the glass, and their mother lies back against the pillows and closes her eyes. Slowly she ceases to breathe, and she is gone.

Stella feels an emptiness envelop her already empty heart, a darkness that not even her sister's arms around her can hold back. She bites down against the pain. The undertakers will be here soon. Her mother will be cremated tomorrow before the two sisters fly back again to go their separate ways.

So that's it, she thinks. No great profound reconciliation, no washing away of old pain, no cleansing miracle. Just the

old lost feeling. Multiplied. Not even a drink is going to fix
this one.

# Ripe Figs

The figs in the back yard ripen from green to dusky purple in the sunshine, the delicate seeds inside transformed into sunset pink.

It's a strange plant, muses Stella, its flowers hidden inside what pretends to be a fruit, but which is an inverted stem, swollen and protective around the concealed blossoms. A single hole at the end allows the fig wasp to creep inside, lay her eggs and die –the flowers fertilised in a beneficial side effect of her suicide. My future fig jam, she thinks, is blessed by the death of a tiny wasp.

In a file in the kitchen, she has her mother's fig jam recipe, in precise handwriting on a faded blue aerogram.

Add figs, honey, and lemon juice to a medium-sized saucepan. Bring to the boil, lower heat and cook for about an hour, until thick; stir frequently to avoid a burnt pot and jam. Add organic (to be honest, her mother didn't specify organic, but this is Melville in the twenty-first century) walnuts and a dash of port and cook for a further ten to fifteen minutes. Pour hot jam into sterilized half-pint jars (or the appropriate metric equivalent), allow to cool, screw cap on and store in a dark cupboard.

To give to friends for Christmas and birthdays, thinks Stella.

Fig jam with dead wasp and walnuts.

# Kathmandu

Stella is grumpy. She reclines on a remarkably comfortable bed, covered with crisp white linen. Dark carved wooden lintels and a handful of wooden gargoyles add an oriental feel to the otherwise white room. But her stomach is sore from the flatulence she builds up on long flights and despite the elegance of the hotel, neither the TV nor the WiFi works – snuffed out by a power outage – and, of course, she didn't bring a book or even a Kindle, relying on TV and/or YouTube to unwind her into sleep.

It's pretty, she admits, but her body clock is out by nearly four hours and sleep eludes her like a snake in long winter grass. The only thing she has on hand to read is a report on the impact of water rights systems on access to water for the poor. Noble, but not tempting after sixteen hours of travel. Although it would put her to sleep.

It should have been fourteen hours if everything had gone smoothly, but, of course, it hadn't. First, they'd been put in a holding pattern above Kathmandu for over half an hour, round and round and round. The first time the Himalayas poked through the clouds, she was thrilled. She'd even thought she could tell which was Everest. I've seen Everest, she'd thought, with childlike glee. Even the third time around she was still excited, but after the fourth slow circle, the Legends taking on bad guys in leaps through time was more interesting than the white mountain tips that rose above the clouds.

After what seemed like hours, they came in to land, but seconds from touch down, the engines roared and they accelerated back up into the sky and back into a holding pattern. The tailwind was above legal limits, the pilot told them. In the dangerous conditions of Kathmandu airport, you can't land if the tailwind exceeds ten knots. So she'd gazed blankly at Everest, still peeking out of the clouds, and turned to the next episode of *Legends*. Another half an hour of circling, and at last they drew up next to the airport building five minutes before the end of the episode.

And then there were the queues. First, for the machine that looked like an ATM and spat out her visa details once she'd typed in her info, well, once she'd waited for the guy in front to plod his way through the several commands. Then there was the queue to pay. Then there was the queue for the immigration official with his scanning machine that rejected her passport three times, until, on the advice of a superior who took ages to arrive, he rebooted his machine, which itself seemed to take forever.

To get from immigration into the baggage area, she had to put her hand luggage through an X-ray machine and step through a metal detector. In case she'd magicked up something lethal on the plane? She pushed and shoved in the unruly line, determined not to lose her place to a group of rudely physical Chinese men. With the press of people and the number of bags shoved higgledy-piggledy onto the conveyor belt, it was unlikely the X-rays would pick up any strange items in the luggage – a feeling borne out by the discovery when she got to her hotel room that she had carried a Bic lighter in her handbag through at least three airport screenings.

Why the hell do I have a lighter in my bag, she wondered. I don't even smoke.

By the time she got to the carousel, the mass of humanity around the small conveyor belt was at least four people thick, interlaced with steel trolleys intertwined like the concrete *dolosse* that hold back the thundering waves on vulnerable coastlines. She couldn't get near to the carousel. As it turned out, by the time her suitcase came around the crowd had thinned – it was the last one to come out from behind the little black curtain. Alone and vulnerable on the empty carousel.

Someone's suitcase has to be last, she thought, trying to be philosophical, or zen, or something – after all, this was Nepal. But a little voice in the back of her very un-zen mind whispered – yeah, but why does it have to be me?

The delays meant that they hit rush-hour traffic, doubled the time it took to get to the hotel. It was a strange trip, the sun like a blurred white-hot disc behind a haze of forest fire smoke and pollution blown up from Bangladesh and India and stopped by the wall of the Himalayas.

She was surprised by how little evidence of the recent massive earthquake there was. The city looked remarkably intact and vibrant. Although she was disconcerted by the electricity cables, strung like dark spaghetti along the streets, tangled into toxic webs on street corners, broken wires dangling like jellyfish tendrils to zap unwary pedestrians.

Back home, she thought, the wires are underground. It leaves the city more open, lighter. And, she chortled, more prone to blackouts from severed cables when municipal workers dig down to fix broken sewer pipes or Heffalump traps, where they dig to repair broken cables. You can't win, she thought. There's good and bad in every situation. Yin and yang. Damn, must be the Nepalese air getting to me already!

So, there she is, in her hotel room, about to reach in desperation for the report, when the phone rings. It's reception, to tell her that the WiFi is back on and the TV is working again.

Thank god, the legal ramifications of water authorisation systems for the poor can wait for another time. First, she needs to explore the ramifications of Nepalese TV. If that doesn't work, maybe she can find an episode of *Would I Lie to You?* that she hasn't watched.

Five minutes later, Stella doesn't know whether to laugh or cry. The TV is not working, as eight channels of snow show her only too clearly. And while her computer claims to be connected to the WiFi, the speed is so slow that emails would go quicker by a runner with a cleft stick. Lee Mack and David Mitchell can't even get the faintest glimpse through cyberspace and onto her screen. The little circle just goes round and round. Round and round. And round and round. She was happier when the Wi-Fi didn't work. At least then she didn't have expectations. This is like tantric sex, only without the pleasure.

She sets her alarm, hopes that she will fall asleep soon enough to wake up somewhat refreshed, and works out, with slight horror, that she will have to drag her body out of sleep at what it thinks will be 4:15 a.m. Right in the middle of the deepest part of sleep. She hates it – waking up in a different time zone with her body aching from the dislocation.

Three hours and forty-five minutes difference from back home she thinks. What an odd decision someone made – to make Nepal fifteen minutes ahead of India. The political ramifications of time zones. Time here is most peculiar, she thinks. If one were to drive due north from India, through Nepal, one would move fifteen minutes ahead as one entered Nepal. Then, a few hundred kilometres farther on (ignoring the difficulties of driving through the Himalayas), one would cross into China and leap ahead four and a quarter hours: from ten in the morning one moment to just after two in the afternoon the next. The huge whole of China runs on Beijing time, some 300 kilometres east of Nepal. Almost as weird as those points around the world where traffic moves from the right-hand side of the road to the left. Peculiar human constructs overlain on a seamless natural world.

She is woken, a few hours of restless sleep later, by the raucous *oompah* of a brass band in the courtyard outside her window. For a moment she lies tangled in the white sheets and duvet, head half buried in the oversize pillow, before she lurches to the window and contemplates the noise and the associated colour and buzz in dismay.

So much for a peaceful morning.

A large white tent has sprouted on the dusty, sparse lawn. White plastic chairs wait in patient rows around a low central stage decorated with huge vases of flowers and a large brass bowl. Butterfly women carry packages and handbags and flutter in glittering saris amongst the chairs while their moth coloured men huddle in groups, smoke and look serious.

A single drum beats out a foot-stomping rhythm, entangled in the whining whistle of a couple of Asian flutes, and the tinny blast of brass wind instruments of unknown name and origin. It is not a rhythm or a key that talks to her Western upbringing, but the tapping feet and swaying hips below her in the increasing crowd under the white tent tell a different story.

Nepalese wedding music turns out to be the theme for the day, Nepalese weddings being of longer duration than the ones she is used to.

That afternoon she sits in an elegant ballroom, midway down the long U-shaped set of tables clad in white satin cloths and adorned with small brass vases of sword fern and snapdragons. It's late afternoon, and at the far end of the room, an elderly man witters on about water in Nepal, his reminiscences and pronouncements insufficiently drowned out by the *thump thump oompah oompah* of the wedding band.

She'd expect them to be exhausted by now, but if anything, the music seems to gather strength as the afternoon wanes. Between the music and the droning speech, her brain has turned to mush and her eyelids threaten to close. She cups a hand behind her ear in the hope that she can focus on the elderly man's words, but the music gets louder and his strong accent smudges his words even further into the background.

She sighs, wishes she could sneak back into her room and write up an overdue report on water quality. As soon as the discussion is over, they will head out into the garden for a cocktail party and she will be expected to mingle and schmooze. Not her favourite occupation.

She sighs again.

# The Journey

She has a few hours to kill before her flight and wanders around Thamel. It is a tourist paradise, or nightmare, depending on your point of view, crammed with tiny shops filled with curios of uncertain provenance and eager faces that encourage her in broken English to buy. She feels pressurised and lonely. Cheap curios are not on her bucket list, and it is not long before she is bored and decides to head back through the narrow, busy streets to the quiet hotel.

She thinks she can remember the way, but the turn that should lead to her hotel leads, instead, into a street she has not been in before. Perhaps if I go down here and left? She curses her dreadful sense of direction.

Just then, as if by magic, a bookstore materialises between the curio shops, and involuntarily, she steps inside. It is tiny, bookshelves cover every inch of wall space, from floor to ceiling, and a great more in between, crammed with every book – fiction and non-fiction – one might ever have wanted to read but haven't had time. How enchanting to find this hidden gem in a narrow street in Kathmandu.

She browses the shelves like a hungry goat, her fingers run over the titles, a smile of astonishment on her lips. Mandela's *Long Walk*, *Karl Marx, His Life* and *Thought*, Steve Biko writing what he likes. This must be the political section.

She squeezes herself through the narrow aisles, past German and French books. *Catcher in the Rye, 1984, Heart of Darkness.* The classics. And then the spiritual stuff.

She is about to turn away when a thin volume catches her eye: *Peace is Every Step.* Perhaps the thought of five days of hiking through the Nepalese hills makes her take it down. Thich Nhat Hanh, Vietnamese Zen master, poet, and peace activist, she reads. Never heard of him.

'As beginning meditators,' she reads, 'we may want to leave the city and go off to the countryside to help close those windows that trouble our spirit. There we can become one with the quiet forest, and rediscover and restore ourselves, without being swept away by the chaos of the "outside world". The fresh and silent woods help us remain in awareness, and when our awareness is well-rooted and we can maintain it without faltering, we may wish to return to the city and remain there, less troubled.'

The words strike a chord, and later that day she tucks the book into her handbag before she sets off for the airport.

The airport buzzes with guides and their clients clad in climbing boots, heavy backpacks, shiny new North Face jackets, and the latest in lightweight, intelligent material hiking shirts and trousers. A smattering of locals fills out the hall.

Stella feels out of place. Why has she chosen to spend five days with no company except a Nepali guide, to hike through the Nepalese hills? She's nervous – the steepness of the so-called foothills has caught her by surprise, and she's not sure that she can go up and down these hills for six hours a day, even with only a light backpack. Why didn't she choose an easier holiday? Sitting in a hotel with a view of Everest, where she could contemplate life while sipping Irish coffee at ten in the morning.

Last night she Whatsapped to Mark that perhaps during the five days, she'd find herself, LOL, but here in the airport, as she waits for the check-in desk to open, she doubts that walking for five days will bring relief from her mother's death, David's suicide, her own inadequacies.

She admits, as tears prick the back of her eyelids, that she will always be a mess. That she will always hang on to the edges of normality by her fingertips, veering between happiness, acceptance, and despair on a roller-coaster ride beyond her control. It will take more than five days of rice, lentils and steep mountains to stop her being a sad, grumpy cow and to bring inner serenity.

She sighs, watches a long-legged young couple, who look fit, elegant and confident. Where did she miss the boat? Where did she turn into a frumpy, middle-aged woman, alone, having lost, somewhere along the road, the bounce in her step, the I-don't-care insouciance of a young woman who trod her own path? Where did she lose her style, her beauty, the thing that made men turn to look, to whistle even, to cross the room to talk to her?

She knows that part of this angst is driven by the uncertainty of the trip ahead; the anxiety of whether she will get onto a plane that has no reserved seats, where it's first come, first served and where you can get left behind in the bustle of others pushing to get on. Or so the stories have been told to her, by amused colleagues. She knows too that this anxiety is driven by the five days of walking ahead and her concerns about the ability of her overweight, undertrained body to cope with the rigours of the hike.

But the knowledge doesn't stop her heart racing, her stomach clenching.

She eyes the clock. Ten minutes before she checks in and tests the apocryphal stories of Yeti Airlines. Look on the bright side, she admonishes herself – maybe you'll see an actual yeti in the next five days!

After a perfunctory pat down by a female official at the security check, she is into the departure lounge where things feel more normal, plenty of ordinary passengers, and several older people, like her, clad in jeans and ordinary t-shirts.

'Tara Air announces that all flights to mountain region are cancelled due to poor visibility. Please return to check-in desk. All inconveniences are highly regretted.'

Confused passengers mill like termites on a broken mound.

Stella walks up to the departure gate.

'Pokhara?' she says.

'Wait,' the young woman behind the counter smiles at her, 'not yet.'

'Not cancelled?' asks Stella.

'No,' she smiles 'not cancelled.'

Stella sighs with relief and returns to the row of metal mesh seats. Next to her sit three elderly Nepalese women in shawls, grey-streaked black hair pulled back into tight buns, Chinese pseudo-leather handbags clutched on their laps. One has a gold stud in her nose and a red patch marked on her forehead. A woollen shawl with the geometric patterns that Stella recognises as Nepalese is wrapped around over one shoulder and under the other arm. She looks patient. Used to waiting. Quiet. Faintly amused.

Stella wonders who they are and where they are going. Wonders to which of the thirty-five ethnic Nepalese groups they belong. Their looks are more Aryan than Mongolian, which seems to be the distinction used here, reflecting southern or northern origins – the Indian subcontinent versus the Chinese land mass.

The elderly lady speaks, to her, presumably in Nepalese, although, to be honest, Stella has no idea what language it is. She smiles and shakes her head. 'I don't speak Nepalese, I don't understand.'

The woman smiles back.

'Pokhara,' Stella says, the name of the town she is heading to being the only thing she can think of.

Recognition lights up the woman's eyes. 'Simikot,' she replies and waves her hand in the air as if Simikot is a realm in the clouds, as well it might be in this mountain kingdom. Stella nods. The women's flight is called and with a smile as timeless as Everest, she waves goodbye and passes out of the door and into the air.

The departure hall empties rapidly, with only the Yeti Air flight still to be called. Excitement begins to tickle Stella's blood vessels and her sense of humour returns. This could be fun, she thinks, and I will be undaunted by the mountains. I can do this, it is all in the head. The legs are OK. It is the head that must hold it together.

Behind her, a group of young French hikers takes selfies, using a small boxy camera which she thinks has some trendy name like 'go pro' or something, but which is too far out of her age paradigm for her to know or care about. She has little to no record of herself in the countries through which she has travelled, even when she hasn't been alone. Instead, she has pictures looking outwards, records of what she has seen, not of being seen.

Hah, she thinks, I haven't even left a legacy of myself in my photographs. I will truly and utterly vanish from the landscape when I go.

# Days in the Mountains

The plane to Pokhara takes thirty people on narrow seats, propellers spinning through the thick white cloud. They could be anywhere, and reports of a small plane that went down in the Nepalese mountains recently flash behind Stella's eyes.

She scrabbles in her bag for paper and a pen, scribbles a quick note to Sandra. 'If something should happen to me, if this plane doesn't make it, remember that I love you, even in my darkest moments. It has largely been a good life. Don't mourn me too much. S.'

She slips the note into her handbag, convinced that no one will ever find it if the plane smacks into a mountain. Just then the wheels come down and the plane dips towards the landing strip. The flight is shorter than she thought, and they touch down with a bump of reality onto the tarmac between smoky ghosts of mountains.

At the Trekking Office, she meets her guide, Sunita. Her sexual preferences are clear. Stella can't imagine that life is easy for lesbians in Nepal – she seems to remember that homosexuality was decriminalised some years previously, but that doesn't mean it is accepted. Look at South Africa, she thinks.

A minibus drops them at the edge of town, and they begin the hike with a short but breath-grabbingly steep uphill slog, and lunch at a villager's house above Pokhara: rice, dhal, green beans and potatoes with a green tomato and coriander relish, much of it homegrown and freshly picked.

'Don't drink the water,' Sunita warns, as she accepts a glass for herself. 'It is not good for tourists.'

The sun is warm on the veranda, and Stella relaxes back against the whitewashed wall and sucks chlorinated water from her camel pack.

'Are you married?' Sunita asks.

Stella shakes her head, too somnolent to open her mouth.

'Lots of women love me,' Sunita confesses with remarkable candour, 'but in Nepal, it is not allowed for women to marry women.'

Stella is curious how much pressure to marry this young woman has had to resist.

'In South Africa,' she responds, fighting a wave of sleepiness, 'gay marriage is legal, but black lesbians are still raped and murdered in some places, just because they are lesbian.'

Sunita looks at her, shocked by the violent nature of South Africa. It is shocking, Stella thinks, bloody shocking and unacceptable. What the hell does it matter who you choose to sleep with? Who does it hurt?

'Come,' says Sunita, 'let's go,' and the hike begins in earnest.

Three hours and ten kilometres later, they are five hundred metres above Pokhara in the small village of Astam.

As Stella drags her weary legs to a seat that overlooks the valley, she passes four young hikers around a table.

Bloody hell, she thinks, that's a South African accent! Ten thousand miles from home, up a mountain, and the only other non-Nepalis around are South African? What's the odds on that?

Above her, a black kite hangs like a shadow puppet in the smoky, diffuse light, the splayed feathers of its wingtips caressing the air.

On the mud-plastered veranda of the house next door, an old woman clad in the bright red of marriage sits cross-legged, shelling dried organic coffee beans by hand, one at a time, to be served, in time, to guests at the eco-village in which Stella is staying. At the table behind her, the South Africans talk Reiki and meridians and their daily yoga practice.

Stella would love to ask if they have come to Nepal to further their spiritual journey or for the exotic beauty of the place. She wonders, not for the first time, what this spiritual quest that so many of her friends and colleagues seem to be on really is.

What is it about this part of the world that Westerners have been coming here for years to find themselves? What do they find here? Does the old woman in red, who cleans coffee beans one by one, have a deeper spiritual wisdom than an old woman who pounds maize in a remote African village? What does she think about, as she counts her passing hours in coffee beans? Is she at peace? Does she live only in the moment as the mindfulness gurus would have us live, or is she anxious, worried, perhaps, about when the gods will shake the mountains again, this time maybe claiming her or her family as victims?

Stella imagines trying to get Sunita to translate the question – do you live in the moment, or do you worry about the future? I'd be worried if I lived here, Stella thinks. The bare soil left behind by landslides stands out starkly on the grassy hillsides. Very worried. She remembers Thich Nhat Hanh in her backpack and wonders if he has answers.

In the grey air, a Himalayan Griffon slides past, turns his head briefly to stare at Stella before moving on to look for smaller prey.

Shanti, wife of Rajesh who runs the eco-village, offers massage, Reiki and reflexology. Stella books a massage and Reiki, hopes it will relieve the spasm that seems to have bound her collarbones to her shoulders in a necklace of pain.

She's good, this butterfly woman in the red embroidered tunic and bottle green trousers, gold chain around her brown throat and red bangles on her wrists. Her hands are practised and strong, her elbows merciless on Stella's back, and she seeks out, unerringly, the points of tension, the locked muscles. It is good pain, and good to be touched. It has been a while since Stella has felt the caring touch of another human being.

Massage over, Shanti holds her hot palms over Stella, works her way over her body, and comes to rest, at last, with her hands folded over Stella's face like a living hot water bottle. There is something meditative about her face cupped in Shanti's strong yet gentle hands. She lies with her eyes closed until a soft voice speaks.

'You felt something with the Reiki?'

Stella grunts, unsure of what to say and what it was she should have felt.

'When I put my hands on your head, your head said I am very full, go away. But your eyes said give me more power. When I wanted to take my hands away they said no, give me more power. Your head, your knees, your feet are strong, but your eyes need more power.'

Certainly, her head is full, but what does it mean that her eyes want more power? Is this a physical thing – a recognition of astigmatism and myopia? Or is this a deeper, more spiritual thing, a recognition that despite her scepticism, Stella is looking for something. Meaning perhaps.

This is where she always starts to feel inadequate – as if Shanti is talking a language she ought to understand but doesn't. Perhaps she just doesn't have the god gene.

A faint hum of traffic and the occasional musical hooter rises from the valley below. Night has fallen and the valley has only a smattering of lights, many of them the headlights of the ceaseless flow of trucks and cars. Up on the hill, Stella has been given a tiny solar light which glows at her side, attracting moths in the general dark.

For a moment, Stella has a rare sense of contentment until the bark of a nearby dog breaks through her calm and irritates her with its incessant monotony.

She sucks on a beer mug of cold Tuborg. Why Danish Tuborg should be available in this remote village is obscure, but its nutty coolness is delightful. Although it is early for bed, if she doesn't retreat soon, she will be forced to kill the neighbour's dog. She downs the last of the Tuborg and retreats to a soft pillow and the sleep of tired muscles.

They set off the next morning after a vegetable omelette and organic coffee, towards Dhampus, the mountain gods still hidden behind the clouds and pollution.

The local school could be a government school in any developing country she has been to – one long double-storey block of classrooms. It has wise sayings painted on its walls: "Learn to listen and then listen to learn." And "He who shows kindness is repaid with love."

Is that why she has not found love, Stella wonders – she is not kind enough? She remembers so many acts not of unkindness, but of not-kindness, where it would have taken so little to be kinder. She wonders how the Mother Theresas of the world can give and give and give and not feel sucked dry.

James argued that it was not altruism or faith but pure selfishness that drove them, as it drives all of us. 'It's just that they get their jollies from helping others,' he said.

Is it as simple as that, she wonders, remembering a study that showed how your level of altruism depended on the size of your amygdala. Clearly, my amygdala is under-developed, she thinks. Mother Theresa and the Dalai Lama must have amygdalas the size of Africa. Or Asia perhaps.

As she steps, as if in a game of hopscotch, from pearl-sheened flagstone to flagstone, she sees that her greatest acts of unkindness are towards herself. There is no one to whom she is as harsh as she is to herself. Is that the lesson of Nepal, that she must be kind to herself? If that's the lesson, then perhaps she doesn't need to walk any further. She's enlightened enough now, she'd like to sit down. And stay sitting down.

Hours later, her thighs aching from hours of uphill climb between birdcalls and flashing wings and dancing butterflies, they arrive in Dhampus and wind their way along flagstone pathways between stone houses. They round a corner and look down into a yard, alight with red roses against the stone wall. A rotund old woman is seated on the paved courtyard, washing pots.

'Please tell her,' Stella says to Sunita, 'that her roses are exquisite, incredibly beautiful.'

The old woman's creased face breaks into a cheeky and beatific grin. 'What about me?' she asks. 'Am I not very beautiful too?'

Yes, they assure her, she is very beautiful too, and it is true – an internal beauty that Stella muses on as they meander down to lunch. The beauty of a woman unscarred by TV images of skeletal celebrities, plastic-surgeried into perfection; of jeans designed for the bodies of hipless boys, not postmenopausal women; of dinner party discussion of low carb, no carb, miracle weight loss and toning regimes. Stella's wardrobe has changed to hide the fat that shields her cracked heart. Layers of deception with her hidden inside. There she goes, judging herself again.

Damn it. Be kind. Be kind.

Her aimless thoughts and the simple act of putting one foot in front of the other carry her through the village to a restaurant where she settles down, alone, under a thatched *lapa* to a strange fusion lunch – traditional Nepalese *momo* dumplings stuffed with cheese, tomato and onion and served with Maggi tomato sauce.

A little boy creeps closer and stares. His face is serious as he skirts the edge of the thatched lunch area and eyes her sideways from under shy lids.

Stella takes a photo of him, shows it to him and watches his face crack into the smile of delight of children around the world when they see their own faces. He giggles and hides behind the tree-fern trunks that hold up thatch and Stella's inner child stirs.

In a moment both conscious and innocent, he comes too close, and she reaches out and tickles his still soft skin. His dusty face lights up with laughter, giggles pour out in a waterfall of clear sound. He squirms away, circles, and once again, with deliberate accident, presents his body close enough for her to tickle. The pure laughter pours out, he squirms away, and the game begins again.

On the veranda of the house, a tiny girl, presumably his sister, screams loud enough to wake the mountains. Her mother hauls her onto her lap to suckle with the casual off-handedness of a busy woman, but the screams continue. Without hesitation, her mother dumps her back onto the floor beside her. The yowls continue while the mother dishes out food for herself and the boy, the little girl caught in a crescendo of frustration that only ends when the mother drags her back onto her lap and silences the screams with her breast.

Maybe, thinks Stella, my expectations of my mother were too high. Maybe, like this mother, she had other things to do too. Maybe she did all she was capable of, gave me everything she could. That it wasn't enough for me is my baggage, not hers. She did what she could. The tears prickle in her throat as she looks out over the roofs to the smoke-hidden mountains beyond.

The houses in this area are built of stone, with slate roofs, each stone tile nailed into place on wooden beams, except for the top row where stone pegs driven through the tiles overlap the crest of the roof. The eaves are held up by intricately carved wooden supports, and she wonders what drives such creativity. The stone of this area is perfect for building – strong enough to build, but easy to split into similar-sized building stones or thin roof tiles.

She realises how humans, as they moved from one place to another, confronted new materials, new options, and used them to find new ways to meet their needs. She speculates whether it is movement that drives creativity, be it early humans travelling into unknown areas, or modern migrants fleeing war or searching for economic opportunity. Just as tectonic activity renews the surface of the earth, perhaps human movement renews creativity?

Her belly contracts in a short bout of silent laughter. It is time to walk again lest she falls too deeply into pop philosophy and grand theory. It is enough to have felt the little boy's chuckle.


That evening, in Badhoure, a grimy pack of cards lies on the table in the dining room of the guesthouse. Stella lays out a game of Solitaire on the white laminate table. Years of childhood holidays at the coast reach out through the greasy surfaces, the physical movement of cards from one line to the next, the counting of three cards from the pack in her hand to add to the pile on the table. It is a long time since she held actual cards in her hands. These days, like people the world over, she plays patience on her cell phone or iPad. As if to confirm the cultural colonialism of Solitaire, Sunita leans forward and moves the red nine onto the black ten. These days, everyone knows how to play Solitaire.

At the beach, they would play endless evenings of cards, while the waves broke, crashed onto the rocks outside and slid back with a sigh, a symphony of water on stone. She would turn from snap and rummy to Solitaire, or *gooi-weg* when her parents retreated behind books, and Sandra annoyed her. She would place and move the cards in a slow meditation driven by the simple logic of suit and number, scratching at sunburn and sand, comforted by the sound of the sea.

This is for you, Sandra, she thinks, setting out six cards face down and one face up. Even if you annoyed the hell out of me, you were there for me when Mum got too much.

Following the ritual, she lays out the next row, five face down and one face up. You stopped me when I tried to run away. I was seven. She lays out the next five cards. I packed some clothes and my favourite doll into my school suitcase. And a packet of biscuits. Lemon creams.

She lays four cards onto the five, three onto the four. You ran after me, pulled the suitcase out of my hands, dragged me back inside. Held me while I cried. She lays down two cards. Mum didn't even notice.

She lays down the final card, face up. The two of hearts.

This game of cards is for you, the one who got all the lucky cards.

The next morning Stella wakes with a familiar sense of sadness deep in her bones. Her hands feel shaky. Her internal water table threatens to spill out through her eyes should she take too deep a breath, or hear too kind a word, so that she will taste salt in the corners of her mouth and have to turn away to snatch back control in the morning mist, before she shudders into humiliating sobs.

She knows this sadness. It stalks her from the shadows, leaps out when she relaxes her guard, cuts the sinews of her control so that she crumbles inwards like a collapsed soufflé. She has felt this too often when she wakes in the morning, spooned into the embrace of sorrow. It takes a herculean effort to drag herself from bed, to paste her smile back onto her face, to wash and comb and primp herself into readiness. The energy it takes to pretend.

Fuck it, thinks Stella, I will come back from this and roar with laughter. But just at this moment, I feel like weeping a little, in a pathetic little foetal ball. But I must walk. One foot in front of another. Along the Nepali 'flat' which goes up and down like my moods and isn't flat at all.

And so, she sets one foot in front of the other and follows Sunita up the wide stone steps built by the Badhoure Youth Club. Up and up, step after step, climbing above the tears, which rise with her, knowing as she walks that this too shall pass. And that this too shall return. Not this moment, but this feeling.

There was a time when she took pills to avoid this. They made her feel topped and tailed, so that only part of her remained, the rather dull, middle part. Since then she has chosen to feel it all, wholly committed to the roller coaster, wholly roller.

Perhaps she is an old soul who experienced great sadness in a previous life and hasn't recovered yet. Or perhaps it is the ghosts of her own past haunting her.

David's slight form drifts through the smoky mist beside her, head down, hands in the pockets of his torn Levis. She reaches out but the smoke shifts and he is gone, back into the haze of his own demons that took him from her all those years ago.

For five days, she barely slept, as she kept watch over him. She knew that at any moment he might shatter and vanish. After five days, she could do no more, her eyelids closed like bank vaults and the world went dark.

And when she awoke hours later, the world was darker still.

His body hung from the curtain rail in his bedroom, his old school tie around his neck – his last, ironic joke. He'd always complained as a kid that school was going to kill him. Finally, it had.

She sat on his bed, held his cold foot for comfort, leant against his leg, while her heart broke into a million splinters that stabbed her chest, her veins, inside her skull. She had no idea how long she sat there, just that there came a time when she knew she had to move. And she became efficient Stella again and shut the bedroom door and phoned an ambulance, the police, his parents, a funeral parlour from the yellow pages, Steve, Mzwi, Rachel, put a notice in the paper, until efficient women and men arrived and took charge.

She feels the splinters prick again. She wishes deeply to be alone, but there is nowhere to be alone in these mountains with a guide, and nowhere David does not follow her. A group of brightly clad women passes them en route to the forest to cut firewood.

'Namaste,' she greets them and presses her hands together, despite her knowledge that Nepalis don't greet strangers. As an African, it feels rude to pass another without greeting. 'Namaste,' they greet back and pass on, chatting, all except one, who asks Sunita something in Nepalese. Sunita shakes her head, dismissing the elderly woman,

'What does she want?' asks Stella.

'Painkillers. She says her knees are sore.'

'On these hills, I'm not surprised!''

'I told her we don't have any.'

'But I do. I have Myprodol. It's amazing.' She scrabbles in her backpack while Sunita calls the old woman back from her slow plod up the hill. Stella holds out two red and green capsules.

'Tell her to take one now and one this evening or tomorrow morning.'

The old woman listens intently, nods and smiles, and returns to her slow plod up the hill. Stella hopes that she will have at least one day free of pain.

As Stella walks on, the smile on the old woman's face melts the splinters of pain, the tears recede, and she just walks, enjoying the rush of endorphins, the tart sweetness of golden Himalayan raspberries, the melody of the great barbet's call in the woods, the flash of butterfly wings, even the strain of her muscles as they lift her body step by strenuous step up the hill.

Time passes, counted in steps and birds calls, until thunder sounds in long, drawn-out drumrolls around the hills – the gods warning them to take shelter. The mist has thickened and falls in cold, wet drops. Lightning flashes in the luminous sky and the thunder is so close that Stella can feel it beat in her chest. With luck, the rain will clear away the smoke and she will see the snow-capped mountain peaks that have lurked above her, unseen, for the past days. Already, in the rain, strange shapes appear in the distance, white on white, but too angular to be clouds.

Have the women that passed in morning heeded the thunderous warning and turned home, or are they still in the forest, cutting firewood with their sharp curved blades and loading it into their bamboo baskets? Or are they walking home, with heavy loads, their feet slipping on the muddy forest paths?

She wonders how the old woman who begged for painkillers is doing, whether her knees feel better, whether she has gathered more wood to carry, on pain-free knees.

Here, it would seem, there are two major maladies: sore knees from heavy loads on steep hills, and stomach cramps from untreated water. She is glad for her middle-class lifestyle that allows her to cocoon herself against inclement weather in house and car, her stash of painkillers, her medical aid, her electric blanket in winter, ice for her gin, WiFi and e-books, and holidays on the wild side.

The guesthouse that night is basic, but clean, run by a Gurung family who, Sunita (Gurung herself) informs her, are the only Nepalis who know how to keep things clean, having been trained by the British while serving in the Ghurkhas.

She sits on the veranda, blasted by a chilly wind, and looks out over the valley towards the north. A tantalising shape threatens to appear in the clouds in front of her – Machapucchre, sacred fishtail mountain, unclimbed and unclimbable. Her eyes strain to make out snow from cloud in a peepshow of temptation.

For a second, the clouds part and Machapucchre stands clear, the proud incarnation of Vishnu, kept safe by religious strictures from the predatory pitons of foreign climbers. Maybe religion has its uses, muses Stella, glad that the massive slab of rock in front of her is virgin, unconquered.

Yesterday, as they climbed through the smoke-veiled hills, in a moment of hubris, she felt on top of the world. Now, looking at Machapucchre and Annapurna behind it, she realises how puny her ups and downs have been despite the groans from her tired thighs. To be honest, she has done little other than shuffle from village to village, Sunita barely breaking a sweat while Stella mopped her dripping face and felt her soaked shirt stick to her back.

And yet, seated on this stone veranda, buffeted by the wind and watching the mountain gods reveal themselves to her, she is truly, almost tearfully, joyous.

The rain has passed, but the wind comes in powerful gusts, ripping dust from the dirt roads and sucking it downhill in ochre clouds. In the valley, the clank of corrugated iron warns of a roof lifted and thrown sideways. At the guesthouse, flat metal sheets covering the walls of the dining room reverberate like orchestral tympani conducted by the wind.

Is the wind a god, or a demon here, Stella wonders, or just a wind? Perhaps a god when it brings the rain, and a demon when it tears off roofs. Perhaps it depends on whether you are talking to a Buddhist, or a Hindu or a Bonist. Perhaps the wind is just a temperamental old cow like me, kind one moment, knocking things down the next.

The guesthouse owner, a fair-skinned Gurung woman, watches the roof of the building with anxious eyes. It is less than a year since a landslide, loosened by the earthquake a few months earlier, vomited from the hillside behind their house while they slept, swept away the walls and cracked her on the head with a rock.

This land is not a stable one, Stella thinks, seeing around her the multiple tracks of landslides, like tears wept by the hill gods, rivulets of bare sorrow torn through the trees. She wonders how one learns to trust again when the very ground is shaken under your feet, understands how the Buddhist idea of the impermanence of all things could take root in this fragile land, and is glad she lives on the ancient stability of the Vaal craton, troubled only by faint shakings from collapsing mines and, if she must be honest, the unsettling turmoil of corrupt politics and violent crime.

The evening is cool after the rain, she sleeps well and wakes refreshed, relaxed and ready for the day's walk. After a steep uphill climb, they settle into a rhythm of up and down, through a patchwork of forest and upland pastures ringed by stone walls that remind her of Scotland, the gentle inquisitive grey and pink faces of domesticated buffalo instead of the russet brown of highland cattle. Their dark-lashed eyes follow her footsteps without fear.

After some hours, Stella feels a great need to sit and be still, not because she is tired, but because she is walking through paradise and wishes, for a moment, to be in it, not passing through.

'Don't just do something, sit there,' says Thich Nhat Hanh, and so she sits on a stone step in the path, in a small glade, releases her backpack, and feels the breeze hit the sweat on her back and how time stands still. Here there is no grumpy, chubby Stella, seated on a stone step, listening and watching. There is only the forest, and she, Stella, at one with the trees, the butterflies, the orchids and the Himalayan Griffon that drifts low above the clearing.

Here, Stella is clear like pure quartz, transparent to the light from this forest. There is no world other than this moment of translucency and this forest dying at every moment and reborn from its own death. She has no idea whether she sits there for a minute or an hour or forever. Perhaps she is still there. Or perhaps the clearing is still in her.

She knows, when she rises and walks on, that she is lighter.

They are chased to Panchase by thunder that bounces around the mountains, the angry roar of the gods. In the village, a group of men with much argument and gesticulation and a certain *rakshi*-lubricated enthusiasm, struggle to replace a roof, ripped off by the wind the previous night – the thunder driving their chaotic efforts, or perhaps the chaos of their efforts. The hastily nailed-down sheets of corrugated iron provide precarious closure against the impending rain.

Next door to the Happy Heart Hotel three men chip stones with sharp-ended hammers and exquisite precision and fit them like jigsaw pieces into thick stone walls, bound together with mud cement. Fingers rendered rough and thick by years of masonry build this delicate artwork. Three Gurung sisters own the Happy Heart Hotel and they have hired three men to build an extra room. Is there luck in threes? Or just chance?

Around the building site lie piles of shale, perhaps twenty million years old, ready to be trimmed and slipped into place in the growing walls. The much thinner slate roof tiles will be layered on later when the walls have reached their full height.

As Stella rests her weary legs under the shade of a painted *lapa*, more stones are delivered, carried in a traditional bamboo basket on the back of a middle-aged woman, held in place by a strap around her forehead. Good god, thinks Stella, there must be at least thirty kilograms in that basket. And I'm tired with only ten on my back.

Lunch, fried noodles and vegetables fresh from the garden, tasting of wood smoke, arrives. As Stella satiates her hunger the woman goes up and down the hill, repeatedly, methodically, like Sisyphus, carrying rocks.

A young man, blue-eyed, full-bearded, but with a shaven head, and a young woman in Nepalese trousers and long hair arrive, hands together, their smiles gentle.

'Namaste.'

Hippies, Stella thinks, twenty-first-century hippies. Not much different from 1970 hippies.

'How-much-tourists,' whispers Sunita. 'The first thing they say is always "how much?".' And true to type, the young woman leans into the kitchen, greets the youngest sister as she stirs a pot over the fire, and asks, 'How much?'

'Three dollars a night.'

'If we stay for a week will you make it two dollars seventy-five.'

Good god, thinks Stella, three dollars is less than a cup of coffee in the USA and you still want to knock it down by a paltry twenty-five cents?

'Three dollars,' the sister responds without a smile. 'Otherwise find somewhere else.'

The hippy wanders off with her gentle smile but floats back later in a haze of hash, boyfriend in tow. They settle down onto the balcony outside their $3 room with instant noodles, tea and vacant stares.

All the while the eldest sister walks up the hill with a basket of rocks, unloads them, and returns down the hill for more. Her efforts seem to add little to the huge pile of stones scattered around the site, but with a sense of amazement, it sinks into Stella's urban consciousness that all of the stones got there this way.

No one drove a bakkie up here and dumped them. No one brought an ox cart of stones up here. Human power, woman power, brought these rocks here.

*Eish!*

'She chooses it,' says Sunita, apparently able to read her mind. 'She prefers it to cooking. Her day starts at dawn cutting forage in the forest for the buffalo cow and her calf and the three goats. Then she swaps the forage in her basket for stones and ferries them until the sun hides behind the western hills.'

It seems to Stella to be a bitter punishment for choosing not to cook. She wonders if the woman's head feels loose, like it might drift off into the clouds, when she takes off the forehead strap at the end of the day and bends to scrub her feet and legs in the outside wash area. Maybe the rocks root her to the ground, stop her from flying away in the thin air, like a Himalayan Griffon. Maybe the rocks are penance for some undeclared sin committed in youthful passion. Maybe it's just how life is here. If you want rocks, you carry them. Full stop.

An ancient crone sweeps the neighbouring yard, her back parallel to the ground, her hands reaching down to pick out bits of rubbish from between the paving stones. When she moves, still bent over, out of the yard and onto the path, sweeping with gentle persistence, Stella understands that the old woman cannot stand upright, condemned by osteoporosis to face the earth forever. Her back aches in sympathy and she straightens up a little.

It is night four of the hike, and Stella is comfortable, as if she has dipped into another world that has welcomed her without question. She is surprised by the thought. No one has been curious about her, no doubt because this is such a popular tourist area. No one has asked if she is married, where she is from, whether she has kids. They are strangers, and pass in disinterested, but not unkind, silence.

She has been granted a superficial snapshot of this life, but she contemplates whether the people here, with their sporadic electricity and no TV, could comprehend her life – days at a computer, nights on YouTube, reading e-books or browsing Showmax; Ubering to the airport; washing her clothes in a fuzzy-logic machine that does everything except iron them; endless hot water thanks to solar energy supported by grid based electricity; a woman to clean the house and do the ironing that the washing machine hasn't yet learned to do, and a man to mow the lawn and plant seedlings in what she likes to imagine as her own organic vegetable garden, although her only engagement with it is to harvest the veggies that he has grown.

She stretches her tired thighs and calves – nothing in Nepal is flat, and her legs have carried her backpack and her chubby belly and breasts up and down for days – and picks up her camera, looks around for interesting shots, new angles on Nepalese village life. Truth be told, there is little village life here outside of the guesthouses. It seems as if there is a policy to keep tourists away from real Nepalese life.

Behind the guesthouse, two men saw tree trunks, harvested from the forest, into planks and beams for the new guesthouse, one on each end of a massive two-handed saw. They slice in common rhythm through the wood, release its warm scent into the afternoon, and produce an enviably straight beam out of their ballet. She clicks a couple of shots, as always, too shy to aim her camera directly at them, lest her lens intrudes into their daily world.

She knows how she would react if someone wandered into her office or her backyard and took shots of her, an exotic bird in its cage gazed at by interested tourists. Why should it be different here? She still takes the pictures, but surreptitiously, so that the pictures are poorly framed, and capture the moment, but not the soul. Occasionally, she is bold enough to ask if she can take the picture. She swallows the occasional rebuff with embarrassment or captures the self-conscious posing, the camera-eager smiles when the answer is yes.

On the roof next door, an elderly man checks the nails in the corrugated iron. He taps each nail and slides gingerly across to the next beam. He slides, she notices, between solar panels and a satellite dish. Behind her camera, she starts to chuckle: that's what keeps the lights and the TV on. What a mistake to think that anyone, anywhere, is no longer connected.

It is dark outside, dark inside. No bedside lamp to switch on, head torch somewhere on the floor beyond the reach of her groping fingers, cell phone switched off and in her backpack. Stella tosses on the tilted bed, uncomfortable and shorn of sleep. Nepal carries no magic cure, after all.

Her anxieties hover around her head, bounce off the overstuffed pillow, bombard her skull, and fight back against the forest peace that she clings to like a drowning cat on a spar of driftwood in a flood. Her mother leans back on a bed covered in a bright yellow tablecloth, eyes open, and waits for Stella to speak, but her tongue is frozen against the roof of her mouth and no words will come.

She wakes again, as the morning light peeps through the wooden shutters, and drags her soul back from a surreal dream in which her naked body was painted like a thinner, negative sepia image of herself. It moved, as if underwater, between busy black and white cartoon creatures come to life against a background of graffiti'd walls, while a second-rate American TV actor, whose name she cannot remember, or, indeed, what she has seen him in, bounded up and down in a ludicrous imitation of a Maasai warrior.

Spray-painted on the wall behind the manic mockery of a Maasai was a portrait of someone she knew, but awake, she can't remember who, just that it distressed her.

What the hell was that about? She reminds herself that she is in a guesthouse in the foothills of the Himalayas, not an anime movie on psychedelic steroids. Unravel that one, dream interpreters! She unkinks her back, swings her feet to the wooden floor, and prepares to go in search of breakfast.

A cup of the Ethiopian coffee she has hauled up hill and down dale in her backpack pushes the dream into the mists and restores her sense of humour. The lightly fried, unleavened Gurung bread, smeared with strawberry jam, brings the final touch of joy to the morning. Today is her last day. She intends to make the most of it.

The hippies join her at the breakfast table, Yuri and Anna, from Russia. He has eyes the colour of ice-melt rivers, and a smile free of guile. He has travelled around for the past ten years, Anna for three, no plan, no map, just going where the moment takes them, a small Russian guitar on his back, a light cloud of *ganja* smoke protecting them.

She wishes for the uncluttered clarity she imagines in his eyes, amused, at the same time, by how easily she projects her desires onto this stranger. Who knows what demons he wrestles, what fears he has run from for ten long years, what bitter memories he carries in his battered backpack. She watches him spread jam on his freshly fried Gurung bread, and something in the turn of his head fires up her synapses.

David, she thinks, it was David's portrait in the dream. Why now? Why after all these years did she dream of David?

The old woman walks past on the flagstone path, returned already from the forest, her bamboo basket filled to the brim with green leaves for the buffalo cow who watches with placid eyes from the shed beside the house. Stella feels lazy and fat, shamed by the diligent women around her, the strong back and legs of the old woman stopping now beside the buffalo shed.

She wonders how old she really is. It is impossible to tell. Yesterday a woman stopped to chat to Sunita as they paused along the path to rest. Sunita gave her a piece of energy bar, which she sucked and mumbled around between her few remaining teeth. Stella asked how old she was.

'She doesn't know,' responded Sunita.

Yes, thought Stella, that makes sense. What does the number of years matter here? What matters is whether you can carry a basket of wood on your back, whether you can bear children, whether you can pick it all up and start again when the mountain shrugs and the houses tumble and the land slides away like melted ice cream.


It is late afternoon by the time Stella tosses her dirty pack onto the floor in the guesthouse and steps under a hot stream of water that washes away the sweat and dust, but not the ache in her legs. Today was downhill. From Panchase to Pokhara. Five hours of downhill on steep flagstone steps and dirt paths. Down and down. Relentlessly down, until Stella wondered if her calf muscles might give up, let go of her taut tendons, and pitch her, legless, down the hillside. It might have been a relief.

As the water flows over her back, she remembers Shanti's comment that her knees were strong. They might be strong, she thinks, but they're bloody sore, a sharp point of pain marks the point of attachment of a tendon, a dull ache inside the joint where the cartilage has worn.

They should be cast in bronze and stuck up on a wall of honour, she thinks. Two chubby brass knees to gaze down on the world and smirk: we carried that lump of lard up hill and down damned steep dale. Gaze upon us and be afraid. Be very afraid.

She sits on the bed to pull on a clean pair of trousers, her legs not bending as she needs them to, and slips on a pair of sandals, her dusty boots discarded in the corner of the room. Down the road and on the right, the receptionist had said, Taal restaurant, a good place for a drink and some food. With a view over the lake.

She waddles down the road since there is no pavement to speak of. Her calves seem to have shrunk into knots of biltong so that emulating a duck is the only way she can walk. Taal resort and restaurant perches on the banks of the lake, with a liberal littering of twenty-something hippies caught in small knots of foreign accents and stories of mountains and travel.

She should have come here thirty years ago, Stella thinks, when she was young and gorgeous and wore flowing kaftans and homemade sandals. She would have fitted in. Now she feels old and dull next to the glowing skins and taut bodies of the young. A world with mirrors has been a shock. For most of five days, she has felt comfortable in her body, ready to stride between the mountains. But as she stepped out of the shower a long mirror reminded her sharply that she was still middle-aged, overweight and dimpled with cellulite.

I came to Nepal, she thought, and I found myself. And what I found was that I am the same person I was when I left South Africa. No better, no worse, and no thinner, despite five days of hiking. Oh, this too, too stubborn flesh!

The spaghetti al fungi is delicious, the smoky taste of mushrooms and cream reviving her energy, the chilled, neon-orange Sex-On-The-Lake pouring its vodka and sugary peach liqueur into her aching calves and her tired mind.

She leans back into the worn cushions in the heavy wooden chair. On Phewa Lake, in each small fishing boat, a single fisher dances a strange choreography as he rows backwards with one oar and feeds out a fine fishing net with the other. In the rainy afternoon, the lake is a pewter plate, and a series of hills step back and back in paler shades of mist behind it.

Oddly, the person in the closest boat seems to be a woman. Stella had assumed it was a male preserve.

A familiar phrase tugs at her ears. Oh, my god, she laughs, not even the music has changed since the 70s. Here comes the bloody sun, little darling, it seems like years since it's been here … Decades, little darling, not just years.

Above the hilltop, Himalayan griffons circle in silence. In some parts of Nepal, they practice sky burials, putting out the bodies of loved ones to be picked to the whiteness of bone by vultures. She likes the idea. Cremation is a waste of energy and burial a waste of space. A sky burial would keep her in the web of life, make her part of those vast, silent wingspans, the exquisite eyesight.

She doubts, somehow, that South African law would allow one to feed human remains to vultures. She imagines the chaos if her will demanded that her corpse be fed to vultures in the Drakensberg.

A sky burial at Mont-Aux-Sources. What an exquisite idea!

A man in worn jeans and flip-flops saunters down the path between the restaurant and the lake. His grey hair is tied back in a ponytail, his head rocks from side to side with the slow rhythm of the super-stoned. He looks old enough to have been a hippy since the 70s. She wonders if he has, indeed, been here since the 70s, or if, like her, he came to find himself in Nepal late in life. She wonders if he has found himself different here, whether he dropped his baggage at the border, or whether, like her, he carries his dead mother, his dead best friend, his broken heart, and his half-forgotten dreams with him wherever he goes.

She sighs and orders another neon-orange Sex-On-The-Lake.

# Glossary

Bakkie (Afrikaans or origin, absorbed into all South African languages) – a small truck, literally, a small container.

Baijiu – clear Chinese spirit distilled from grain, barley, peas or rice with the kick of an angry mule, used for toasts at meals to show respect to fellow diners.

Bloubos (Afrikaans) – Diospyros *lycoides*, a South African shrub or small tree. The literal translation means blue bush, although there is little blue about it. The flowers are creamy yellow, the leaves green, and the fruit red.

Boerewors (Afrikaans) – spiced meat sausage; literally farmers' sausage.

Bunna (Amharic) - coffee; Ethiopia is where coffee Arabica originates from.

Chakalaka – spicy South African relish made with onions, tomatoes, chillies, garlic, ginger, curry powder, green peppers, red peppers, and/or beans.

Dankie (Afrikaans) – thank you.

Doek (Afrikaans) – a scarf worn around the head by African women.

Dolosse (Afrikaans) – huge (as in up to 80 tonnes) pieces of reinforced concrete in the shape of an axis with two end T-bars at right angles to each other, used in large numbers to stabilize coastal areas. Invented in South Africa in 1963.

Dorp (Afrikaans) – a small town.

Eish! (South African slang) – an exclamation of surprise, horror, excitement, awe, and just about anything else you want it to express.

Gambai – the Chinese equivalent of 'bottoms up', generally leading to a dreadful hangover the next day.

Ganja (Hindi) – the dreaded weed, *Cannabis indica.*

Gogga (Afrikaans word absorbed into English) – an insect. Gooi-weg (Afrikaans) – a card game played by one person, literally meaning throwaway.

Hadeda – a hadeda ibis (*Bostrychia hagedash*) a large bird with iridescent shoulder patches, a long curved bill, and the cry of a strangled donkey.

Injera (Amharic) – delicious Ethiopian flatbread made from indigenous teff flour. It has a slightly sour taste and a unique, spongy texture.

katjiepiering (Afrikaans) – *Gardenia volkensii*, or Transvaal Gardenia, an indigenous South African gardenia with fragrant white flowers that turn a creamy yellow as they age; literally, kitten-saucer.

Khat (Arabic) - *Catha edulis*, a flowering plant found in the Horn of Africa and the Arabian Peninsula, which contains an amphetamine-like stimulant (cathinone). It is chewed to produce a state of euphoria. It has been used as a stimulant in that region for thousands of years.

Klap (Afrikaans) – smack.

Kraal (Afrikaans) – a traditional grouping of African huts, usually surrounded by a fence or wall of some sort.

Kudu (isiXhosa – iqudu) – a large South African antelope known for its ability to jump over high fences and for making very tasty biltong (dried, spiced meat).

Kufi (from Arabic kūfīya) – a round, brimless cap.

Kurta (from Urdu and Persian kurtah) – a long, generally cotton, shirt, originating from the Indian subcontinent.

Lapa – the South African name for a structure with a thatched roof held up on wooden poles; from the seSotho word for homestead.

Matatu (Swahili, short for 'mapeni mutate' 'thirty cents', a flat fare charged in the early 1960s) minibus taxis in which millions of Africans risk their lives daily to get to around in the absence of functional public transport systems.

Mealie (Afrikaans) – maize, corncob, from the Afrikaans, mielie, which appears to come from the Portuguese, milho, which comes from the Latin, milium. And so, language maps out colonial histories.

Momo (Tibetan) – a stuffed dumpling, usually steamed, and traditionally filled with meat or vegetables.

Pampoen (Afrikaans) – literally, a pumpkin; in slang an idiot (Afrikaans of origin).

Potjie (Afrikaans) –meal of meat and vegetables traditionally slow-cooked in a three-legged cast iron pot over an open fire.

Rakshi (Nepalese) – a spirit distilled from millet or rice, like baiju, it has something of a kick.

Sangoma (Zulu) – a traditional healer, particularly one who uses divination for healing.

Shiro – Ethiopian spicy chickpea paste, usually eaten with injera.

Skop, skiet en donner (Afrikaans) – literally, kick, shoot and beat up – generally referring to violent and melodramatic action movies.

Skoroskoro (township slang) – a run-down, falling apart car.

Takkies (South African slang) – sports shoes, trainers, sneakers.

Tannie (Afrikaans) – aunt, used as a polite term for older women by Afrikaans-speaking youth.

Tokoloshe (Zulu) – a mischievous and somewhat evil pintsized water spirit that becomes invisible by drinking water and that is used by nasty people to cause trouble for others.

*Toxoplasma gondii* – a single-celled parasite that can do weird things to the brain – but relax, in most infected humans there are no symptoms …

Uhuru (Swahili) – literally, freedom.

Warrelwind (Afrikaans) – whirlwind.

# Acknowledgements

A long life journey has brought me to this book, and many people and places have stuck their fingers into the pot, each subtly, or not so subtly, adding to the flavour. I owe a big debt of gratitude to the organisations that funded my international travel (as part of my day job), and as an unintended consequence, have shaped this book. It was never an output in their log frames, but I hope they appreciate it!

Frank Meintjies has been a nurturing critic of my writing over many years.

Kerryjane Gutteridge, Sheena Stannard, Renee Bonorchis, Alana Potter, Barbara van Koppen read the book and variously laughed, commented, advised, drank gin and encouraged me to continue. Jayne Southern mixed the attention to detail of an excellent editor with the sense of humour of a mensch to take the manuscript to another level.

Then there's Monde, my teacher of patience, and a courageous creative spirit, encouraging me by example, to be better.

# About the Author

Barbara has written creatively pretty much since she could write, but what she writes has become more sophisticated and eclectic as she has staggered through the vicissitudes of life towards the final curtain. She has written poetry, plays, fiction and non-fiction works, and edited two books, *A Snake with Ice Water* and *Transforming Water Management in South Africa: Designing and Implementing a New Policy Framework*. She has published poetry in anthologies and journals, has performed her poetry live in various venues, and had a play, *Endangered Species*, performed in Johannesburg, London, the Edinburgh Festival, Glasgow and the Netherlands. In addition to those already mentioned, her published works include *The Gossiping Grass*, a children's story published by Shuter and Shooter, a collection of writings by and interviews with women about their experiences in prison, published by COSAW and *My Spirit is Not Banned*, a biography of the South African activist, Frances Baard, published by Zimbabwe Publishing House.

Barbara has written various journal articles, papers, reports and given numerous presentations in various parts of the world on the subject of water management in developing countries, with a particular focus on how it affects poor women and men.

She carries the dust of Africa in her heart and on her shoes, whether the small-town dust of Pietermaritzburg, where she grew up, the urban grime of Johannesburg where she lived for about 20 years and where she still hangs out for fun, or the more sedate, capital city dust of Pretoria where she now lives and works. She has been blessed with an amazingly talented son, Indigo, rock guitarist, singer and songwriter, who has taught her more about life and music than she could ever have imagined.

# Also by this author ...

A Snake with Ice Water

Transforming Water Management in South Africa: Designing and Implementing a New Policy Framework

Endangered Species (a play)

The Gossiping Grass (a children's book)

My Spirit is Not Banned (a biography of the South African activist, Frances Baard)

Ralph Iron Publishers